THE HOLLOWS

A MIDNIGHT GUNN NOVEL #1

C. L. MONAGHAN

For Ednah

PROLOGUE: LONDON, NOVEMBER 1835

Her screams rent through the air, cutting Josiah to his very core, every scream like a physical blow. She was in agony and had been for hours now, and there seemed to be no end to it. He continued to pace the corridor, listening for any sign it was over. The rhythmic thud of his footsteps was muffled by the thick wool rug and kept time with the ticking of the grand clock on the landing.

The door swung open. Spinning around in earnest, he looked hopeful, but it was just the servant running past with yet another bowl of blood-soaked rags. Josiah cursed and made toward the heavy oak-panelled door to listen. Nothing but ragged moans and intermittent, exhausted screams reached him. How much more could she take?

He returned to his pacing, noticing the natural light was dulling, it was almost time for the eclipse.

"More light!" He heard the doctor yell, "I need more light dammit!" The housekeeper burst through door shouting instructions to whoever was listening to fetch candles and lanterns. Not for the first time did he wish he had installed gas lighting; waiting for candles wasted precious time. People rushed back and forth with hurried purpose, leaving him feeling utterly useless. It was his job to protect her and yet he could do nothing.

Glancing nervously toward the large arched window atop the grand staircase, Josiah noticed the light had almost disappeared. Fretting that the doctor wouldn't be able to see clearly enough to minimise any risk, his pacing halted abruptly. All had fallen silent behind the oak door. The rushing around of bodies had ceased, leaving him stranded in limbo in the lonely corridor of darkening shadows. He glanced again at the window, all traces of sunlight had disappeared, only an unearthly twilight remained. It was 10.30 in the morning and the grand clock rang out the half hour, its chime ominous, almost prophetic. As the last echoes of sound were swallowed by the strange and eerie half-light, a warbling cry pierced the air.

The cry was his signal to move.

"Congratulations Josiah, you have a son." The doctor greeted him with a half-hearted congratulatory smile. He looked dishevelled and sweaty. The fire in the bedroom was raging and threw out an almost unbearable heat. The housekeeper shuffled off to the dressing room, cooing softly at a wriggling bundle of flesh and rags. Josiah looked toward his wife but was not prepared for the shock of it.

"Is she even conscious?" He did not try to disguise the worry in his voice, she was his life and she lay in blood and tatters before him.

"She's exhausted Josiah, it was an extremely difficult birth. The baby was breech and she has lost a lot of blood."

"Will she recover?" He choked, afraid of the answer. The good doctor patted Josiah's arm sympathetically,

"She's in the Lord's hands now. All you can do is pray."

"And my son?"

"He is well and whole, come and see." The doctor indicated for Josiah to follow him to the dressing room but Josiah shook his head.

"Not yet, I must tend to my wife first." Anna, the chamber maid, stood anxiously in the room, wringing her hands. Josiah waved her forward and she scurried over to him and bobbed a quick curtsey. "Fetch clean sheets and a fresh nightgown for your mistress, and a jug of honeyed water; she will be thirsty and the honey will restore her energy. Ask Daisy to come and help you change her." Anna bobbed again and hurried out of the room, set on her master's mission. Josiah turned back to his wife. Placing his hand tenderly on her forehead, he swept away a strand of hair that clung to it and leaned in to kiss the spot where his hand had just been.

"We have a son my Josephine, do you hear that? A son! You must fight now, he will need you... we both will." Josiah stood and nodded at the doctor, following him to his wife's dressing room where Mrs. Henshaw, the housekeeper, vigorously rubbed at the howling babe with fresh rags to clean him.

"He's a fair pair of lungs on him sir, and a wriggler too," she smiled, "I'm about to bathe him and swaddle him. Would you like to hold him first sir?"

"May I?" Josiah was uncertain what the correct procedure may be, this was his firstborn babe and he had no idea if it was permitted. Mrs. Henshaw chuckled,

"No need to be asking permission from me sir, he is your son." Josiah glanced at the doctor,

"Is it safe? He will not ail?"

"Perfectly safe Josiah."

Mrs. Henshaw deftly wrapped the babe in a small sheet, his thick shock of black hair poking out, and handed the bundle to Josiah.

"Now sir, cradle him so...in the crook of your arm see? Hold his head up...that's it."

"He is strong," Josiah chuckled, "see how he wriggles!" Salty droplets of pride prickled the corner of his eyes. He hadn't known such love was ever possible. The love he felt for his wife was as strong and heartfelt, but that had been cultivated over time. The instant bonding of father and son took him completely by surprise and in that instant, he knew he had found his life's purpose.

"Isn't he beautiful sir?" Mrs. Henshaw's heart was lost already, Josiah could tell.

"He will be loved indeed Mrs. Henshaw." The sheet slipped a little from the babe's head to reveal a thick mop of jet black hair, just like his own. He studied the wriggling, caterwauling child in detail. He had Josephine's nose and look, but his brow and chin. He had yet to see the babe's eyes because the child still cried but then he remembered his wife telling him that all babies were born with blue eyes and only changed colour as they grew.

"He's a special one indeed. I must bathe him now sir, if you please?" Mrs. Henshaw held out her arms for the babe. "Has he a name yet sir?"

"No, Lady Gunn and I have made a list but I feel I should wait for her to decide." Josiah said as he handed back his son.

"Very well, Sir. I shall call him little master until then." she said, smiling affectionately. She expertly cradled the little master in one arm after unravelling him from the sheet. A large ceramic bowl sat in readiness on the nightstand to bathe him in. Mrs. Henshaw dipped her elbow in the water to test the temperature and gently lowered the little plump, pink body in. The warm water instantly soothed and quieted him, his squealing changed to soft noises of contentment.

"May I have a word?" the doctor asked and stepped to one

side with Josiah. "Your son is healthy but I must advise you to find a wet nurse and fast. He will need nourishment and I fear your wife is too weak to accomplish the task." Josiah nodded and called for Anna,

"Her ladyship is all settled now, sir." Anna informed him.

"Thank you, Anna. Now I must ask you to send word out for a wet nurse immediately; have you knowledge of where to find one?"

"Yes sir, Mrs. Henshaw has already given us a list of names, just in case you'd be needing one."

"Excellent, you may go then." Josiah dismissed Anna who scurried off to carry out her task. "What would I do without you Mrs. Henshaw?"

"Not my first birthing your Lordship and probably not my last." She said matter-of-factly, dipping a sponge into the water she began scrubbing at a spot on the little master's chest then gasped and stepped back a touch, almost letting the child slip from her gasp. "The merciful Lord no!"

"What? What is it?" Josiah demanded, dashing to the bowl where his newborn son still gurgled contentedly. The doctor followed in haste, fearing some deformity he had missed in the stress of the birth and dim light.

"He's been marked sir! I thought it was just dried blood but it wouldn't scrub off, look here!" She pointed to a black mark on the left side of his son's chest. Josiah squinted and leaned closer; it was hard to see in such dim light. Although the total eclipse had only lasted for four minutes, it was still in its dying throes and had not yet returned to full sunlight. Only two candles burned in the dressing room.

"No fear, it's only a birth mark," said the doctor a little too dismissively. Josiah studied it more closely. It was spine chillingly clear that this was no ordinary birthmark and he instinctively crossed himself. Mrs. Henshaw whispered,

"Is it the devils mark, sir? Surely not for such a beautiful babe?"

"No," Josiah replied, the finality in his tone belying the tingle of fear and superstition that crept up his spine. "It is as the doctor says, just a birthmark...albeit an oddly shaped one," he added.

"As you say, sir," Mrs. Henshaw replied rather hesitantly and continued to bathe the boy dutifully.

The daylight finally began to seep back in through the windows, masking the tinge of doubt that had marred the birth of his firstborn. The return of the bright sunshine and crisp November day radiated with hope for a new chapter in his life. Josiah breathed the light into his body.

Hours passed, and a wet nurse arrived. She was briefed on her duties by the ever-organised Mrs. Henshaw, the little master now lay peacefully sleeping in his crib beside his ailing mother. Anna had brought him a tray of food and refreshing tea but it had tasted dry and bland in his mouth. He had no appetite while his beloved wife lay fretful and barely conscious, still unaware that she had produced a son and heir. The doctor had left with a prayer and instructions to keep Josephine warm and fed with honeyed water, and to send for him if anything changed. Daisy came in some time later to stoke the fire in the already stifling bedchamber and Josiah had relieved himself of all his clothing aside from his trousers and undershirt. He refused to leave his wife's bedside until she awakened and so Anna had brought him a fresh shirt, neatly folded and placed on the chair for his convenience. At his request they had left him alone for the most part, and only disturbed him for necessities.

It wasn't until the clock struck 11.30pm that Josephine regained some lucidity and managed to speak.

"Josiah?" she croaked. He was by her side in an instant, his hand clasped hers.

"Josie, you're awake! Thank God," he said, kissing her hand, "Do you feel better my love? Do you need anything?"

"Thirsty," was all she could manage. Josiah dutifully brought the honeyed water to her lips so she could drink. He replaced the cup and held her hand again, excited to tell her the news.

"You did it, Josephine, we have a boy...and he is beautiful!" Again, he felt the tell-tale tears of pride. Josephine's painfully pale face shone with hope and joy,

"Let me see him." She struggled to sit and Josiah helped her, propping her up with pillows. He carefully scooped up the sleeping baby and proudly handed his wife their son.

"Oh Josiah, look! Look at him, he is perfect." Joy radiated from her and she seemed to draw momentary strength from the presence of the babe in her arms.

They sat together for a few precious moments, despite his wife's weakened state she petted and cooed over her son with trembling hands and shaking voice.

"What shall we name him my love? I waited for you so we could choose together." Josephine smiled weakly at her husband in gratitude for his considerate gesture.

"Something grand," she whispered.

"He is certainly deserving of grandeur, he arrived in such an extraordinary manner."

Josephine sighed heavily, her eyelids fluttering. A sheen of sweat clung to her clammy skin. Josiah felt her forehead; she was feverish.

"Anna!" The chambermaid came running.

"Yes, sir?"

"Send for the doctor, now!" Anna didn't bother to curtsey, acknowledging the urgency of the request, she shot from the room calling loudly for the footman.

"Josiah...open the window...please?"

"The doctor advised you be kept warm, dearest..."

"Please, Josiah. I want to see it." Josiah was momentarily baffled but carried out his wife's wish. He drew back the heavy curtains and the night sky revealed itself to them both. That's when he saw it; the bright tailed light in the clear, black November sky – Halley's comet.

"The window." Josephine said. Josiah unlocked the latch and threw open the window, the last barrier between them and the chill air.

"It's beautiful," Josephine declared. Josiah had to agree. What an extraordinary day it had been. Their son had been born at the height of a solar eclipse and on the very same day Halley's comet blazed a trail through the sky. Josiah had to wonder if it were a beacon of hope or an omen of tragedy.

The grand clock began to strike the first of twelve chimes to ring in the new day. The sheer celestial majesty of it all almost overcame him and Josiah grasped the window ledge. Leaning out, he breathed in deeply the crisp, chill air, filling his lungs and ridding himself of the stagnant heat of the bedroom.

"What shall we name him?" he asked again, returning to his wife's bedside. Josephine's hold on her son had weakened and she struggled to keep him from slipping down the bedcovers. Josiah, rather than remove their son from her arms, held him in place for her so that she may cradle him longer. The grand clock struck twelve.

"Midnight." Josephine's answer came swift and sure, with one last fighting breath to be strong for her son.

"Midnight it shall be then." Josiah's voice broke and he let the tears fall as his beloved wife slipped away, gracefully and peacefully, still cradling her sleeping babe.

1

BLACKFRIARS 1860

"Gunn's here sir," Constable Rowe whispered in his superior's ear. Detective Inspector Arthur Gredge gave a slight nod in acknowledgment and cleared his throat.

"Right, let's have this area cleared!" He shouted and two of the Southwark bobbies started ushering away the crowd of locals that had gathered at the scene. Gredge waited until he and Rowe were alone.

"Fetch him in...and make sure no one sees him and no one comes near." Rowe nodded and slipped off to carry out his superior's instructions. Smoothing down his moustache, Arthur looked over the scene while he waited. The small enclosed alley off Blackfriars Road was dank and dark, it reeked of piss and vomit where drunken revellers had relieved themselves. Dumped in the corner, grotesquely arranged in the great piles of filth and rubbish, with only the rats for company, was the body of Miss Emeline Rowbotham. This one *was* a body; he had checked for a pulse and there was none. The others were still alive...sort of; Miss Rowbotham was victim number eight. Arthur was convinced the cases were all linked but there were a few differences that made this case stand out; this victim was dead, this victim was from a prominent family, and this time... there was a witness.

Arthur shivered unintentionally. The shadows in the alley seemed to spread, growing blacker by the second. He turned towards the alley entrance which now looked like a big black hole. He heard no footsteps, the shadows seemed to swallow the sound.

"Detective Inspector Gredge, we really should stop meeting like this, people will talk," came the droll and alarmingly close voice through the darkness.

"Jesus Midnight, I wish you wouldn't do that."

"Did I make your heart flutter? I am flattered."

"Funny," Arthur rolled his eyes. "I was going to ask if anyone saw you but seeing as I can't rightly see my own hand in front of my face at present..." He left the statement open, knowing Midnight would understand his meaning. A low chuckle reverberated off the brick walls.

"You did tell the constable to make sure no one saw me enter so..."

"You don't think that crowd would notice a bloody great dark shadow appearing from nowhere?"

"You'd be surprised what people let slip past their conscious minds Arthur. They'll most likely pass it off as a trick of the light, a cloud covering the moon... I wouldn't worry about it."

The darkness receded a little to reveal the imposing hooded figure of the man Arthur knew as Midnight Gunn. Arthur had been acquainted with Midnight for a few years now, but he only called upon him when it was necessary. Midnight mostly liked to be left alone although Arthur often got the eerie feeling that he was around, lurking in the shadows, keeping his ear to the ground. It never seemed to take him long to arrive when he called for him.

"So, I take it there is a reason you asked me to come?" Midnight said.

"Body, in the corner there," Arthur pointed. "Miss Emeline Rowbotham, reported missing by her family earlier this evening, found about an hour ago by someone taking a leak. He also happens to be witness to the act. Stroke of luck on that point," he added, "although I'm not sure how reliable he is, blind drunk and blathering on about...well, you'll no doubt see when you do your *thing.*" Arthur cringed. That was a mistake and he knew it immediately. Midnight hated it when he openly referred to his *special skill.* He risked a glance at his colleague and wished he hadn't. Midnight's ice blue eyes blazed with anger and the shadows began to creep back into the alley. "Look, I didn't bloody mean to... you know, mention *it.* I just..."

"Need me to do my *thing,*" Midnight hissed through clenched teeth. The inspector seemed to shrink from him. "Better let me get on with *it* then."

Gredge retreated down towards the alley entrance. He might have cocked up by mentioning Gunn's special talent but he wasn't about to stick around and watch. He'd made that mistake once before and he still had nightmares about it. Reanimating the dead was unholy and wrong, but sometimes it was necessary.

Midnight waited for the Inspector to retreat before he began. He never liked an audience, it made people... uncomfortable. Who could blame them, when he felt the same way? He took a deep breath and centred himself. He flexed his fingers readying them for what he was about to do. This was a dark act and so it followed that he needed to draw energy from the shadows. As luck would have it, there were plenty of those in this stinking alley. A few strides and he stood in front of the corpse of Emeline Rowbotham. He knew she was dead, he could smell it – another of his special skills. Midnight hated the dark half of himself; he preferred his other, lighter side but the darkness always seemed to prevail. There were more shadows in this world than there was light and, more call for his dark talents. If he could use them to help solve a murder then he could at least find solace in that.

Emeline was a pretty name, it suited her. Her blonde curls, now in disarray, fell about her face, framing her delicate features. Her forget-me-not blue eyes were open and her rosebud lips were slightly parted. She looked like a porcelain doll – perfect aside from the bruising that had started to appear on her throat. It looked like an ordinary case of strangulation, but Midnight knew the Inspector must've suspected something more or he wouldn't have asked for his help.

He could feel the shadows pulsing, eager to come to him and so he let them in. He could control the shadows in different ways; he could move and manipulate them to conceal himself, as he had done in the alley with Arthur, and he could pull them inside himself, harnessing their energy to enhance his skills. This particular skill was the one he hated; he could reanimate the dead. Only for a few seconds at a time but, in this instance, it gave him a glimpse of a person's final moments. Most useful when trying to solve a murder.

He drew in the shadows from the alley. They drained from the corners and crevices like water from a sink, swirling and merging together in one dark mass as he pulled them inside himself. The pain of it was almost unbearable; like a million needles tearing at his flesh from the inside. He grunted at first contact but quickly regained the semblance of control he had learned over the years. The sooner he got this over with the better. Midnight stepped towards the girl and crouched over her inert body. Touching his hand to her forehead he reached out and probed her memories. Fast moving, unintelligible images and sounds that were her life flashed through his mind until they began to slow. The newest memories were always the clearest, although it was possible for him to see further into a person's past; the older the memory the blurrier it appeared to him. He waited for the moment of her death to come to him. He never had to wait long; it was as if he and death were old friends and death was eager to show off his newly claimed prize.

The scene played out in his mind. It was pitch black in the alley, late at night. As usual, he was watching through the victim's eyes. He could feel hands around his throat, choking the life out of him. His lungs burned and his eyes watered but he tried to fight back. The corpse of Emeline Rowbotham began to twitch and jerk; choking sounds came from her cold lips. Midnight could see nothing but darkness and the silhouette of the attacker in front of him. The attacker's eyes glowed a bright, unnatural red and he knew then why Arthur had called for him. The killer was not human.

Midnight let go of Emeline and her body went still. He pushed at the shadows, forcing them from his body and back into the alley where they waited, sated for now but always watching.

Midnight watched as Miss Rowbotham's body stilled, then he gently closed her eyes and stroked her face. She had seen enough horror. Tentative footsteps behind him prompted him to speak.

"You were right to call for me."

"The witness was correct then? A red-eyed demon is the killer?" Arthur said.

"Something of that nature... but I will need to question the witness."

"Of course. Constable Rowe already took his statement but you can question him yourself if you feel it's necessary."

"Where is he?" asked Midnight. Inspector Gredge sighed.

"Waiting back in the pub, I'm afraid. One of the Southwark men is keeping an eye on him. Thought you'd probably want to talk to him. Although, he was half cut so lord knows what state he's in by now."

They made their way out of the alley while Constable Rowe came back to supervise clearing the crime scene and Arthur gave instructions to have the body taken to the resurrection men.

The two men found the witness siting at the back of the pub with a Southwark Bobby, calming his nerves with a mug of cider. By the looks of him he'd had several mugs before and since the incident in the alley.

"Jimmy Cartwright, we need you to go over your statement again." Jimmy's head wobbled and he began to protest until he looked up and saw Midnight, then he shrank a little in his seat.

"Who you then? I already gave me statement, what you wantin' another for? I ain't done nuffink wrong and I wants to go 'ome!" The nervousness in his voice contradicted his attempt at defiance. He was scared – Midnight sensed the fear rolling off the man, not because he was afraid of him but afraid of what he'd seen. Midnight pulled up a chair and sat opposite Jimmy. He pulled in a little stream of energy from the flame of the candle that puttered in the wall sconce, and placed his hand on Jimmy's arm. It had an instant calming effect, Jimmy's hands stopped shaking and he looked up at Midnight, "You that wants to know, is it?"

"Yes, tell me what you saw." Midnight said gently

"I went for a piss in the alley there and heard noises see, don't usually pay attention 'cause there's all sorts what goes on in alleys. I thought it was just one o' the dollymops with a fella like but then I saw she was dressed all smart an' all. An' then I saw the...the..." Jimmy shivered and crossed himself before he continued, "*thing* what was killin' her." He crouched forward over the table and lowered his voice, "'T'weren't human, I can tell you that much. Never seen nuffink' like it." Jimmy shivered again.

"Can you describe the creature?"

"Yes sir, it was tall and wore a dark cloak with an 'ood so as to 'ide its 'ideous face." Jimmy said dramatically, "Its 'ands were made of metal, big claws an' all. Then there was them eyes... ugh... them eyes glowed devilish red. S'unnatural, unholy it is. Should've seen it leap clear out the alley when it spotted me! I tell ya, I thought I was a goner when it looked at me."

"It jumped out of the alley?" Midnight asked.

"Clear out sir, in one leap! I hopes you catch it, I don't fancy running in to the bloody devil again."

"Thank you Jimmy, you've been most helpful." Gredge and Gunn rose from the table but Jimmy caught hold of the inspector's coat sleeve.

"'Ere! Ain't there no reward for an 'elpful citizen these days governor? I put me life at risk I did." Jimmy looked hopeful as Inspector Gredge put his hand in his pocket and pulled out a coin.

"For your trouble Mr. Cartwright."

Jimmy grinned, showing off his blackened teeth, swept up the coin and went straight to the bar to order another mug of cider. Gunn and Gredge made their way back outside towards the alley where the cart had arrived to transport the body of Miss Rowbotham.

"I need to visit the family and inform them of the bad news," said Arthur. "Any thoughts as to what killed her? I need something to tell them."

"I'm not sure yet. What aren't you telling me?"

"How do you do that?" Arthur shook his head. "Look, I didn't want to say until you'd seen the body but... there's been a spate of ... *bodies* turning up. None like the lady here. Seven others so far as we know but they're. well... not dead, at least not physically, but I'm sure they're linked somehow."

"How so?"

"All roughly in the same area. Strangulation marks round the neck but no other physical injuries. Up till now they all survived... though by the state of them it'd probably be better if they hadn't." Arthur added.

"What's wrong with them?" Midnight was curious now, he hadn't had a decent case to investigate for a while. He wished Arthur had contacted him earlier but until Jimmy Cartwright's witness statement there hadn't been any evidence to indicate anything supernatural. Arthur scratched his chin, debating how best to describe the condition of the other victims,

"Well, none of them speak or move of their own accord. but I'm told they will eat and drink and relieve themselves when instructed. It's like they're alive but not, if that makes any sense?"

"Where are they? I need to see them."

"Saint Thomas's. Nowhere else to put them, they're not gentry like this one," Arthur said, indicating to the covered body of Miss Rowbotham on the cart. "No families to look after them at home."

"Can you meet me there later today?"

"I'll see you in about two hours. I've got to visit the Rowbotham's first and fill in some paperwork."

Midnight nodded and turned to walk away. He slipped into the dawn shadows and was gone, leaving Arthur to wonder how he always managed to appear and disappear in the blink of an eye.

2

ST THOMAS'

Midnight walked with slow and measured steps to the public ward at St Thomas' Hospital. The harsh aroma of disinfectant failed to mask the stench of soiled bed sheets but nevertheless, he took the time to look over each of the seven patients in the mixed ward.

"I thought you said they were able to function? They're lying in their own urine." Midnight turned to Arthur, incredulous at the state of the ward and its inhabitants.

"They can when someone tells them to but there aren't enough nurses to look after all of them. The Matron said they're very understaffed." Arthur paused and scuffed the toe of his boot on the floor. He wasn't sure why he felt guilty under the scrutiny of his colleague but he did. Midnight had a way of making you feel responsible for things that were beyond your control. It was one of the things Arthur liked about him – his innate sense of what was morally right. He could scare the tail off a horse, mind you, but the man had morals and Arthur respected that. "Can you see anything yet? There has to be something to link them."

"So far four of the women have shown me much the same:

strangulation, red eyes... I can glean little else from their last moments." Midnight stopped in front of the bed of the fifth victim. Pity quickly followed by rage gripped him so hard he felt his chest constrict as the anger coiled inside him. The few shadows that lurked in the corners of the ward leaped excitedly, eager to be called upon, but he fought them back with ease, grateful that the ward windows let in enough light to quieten the dark... this time.

He stepped closer to the tiny limp body of a little girl, her small skeletal frame barely visible under the stiff sheet and itchy blanket. He judged her to be no more than seven or eight years old, a half-starved wretch of a thing whose left arm ended in a bony stump at the wrist. She was an amputee and poor as a church mouse by the look of her.

"Polly's her name." Arthur said. "She's an orphan, we don't know her surname but the other kids said she sold matches down by the dockyard. A gentleman and a group of sailors found her. They thought she'd frozen to death at first. It's not uncommon. Tragic though," he added quickly as he caught the twitch in Midnight's jaw.

"Polly." The child's name fell from Midnight's lips like a blessing, barely a whisper but uttered with such purpose and determination it sent chills through Arthur and he shivered. The room appeared to grow brighter just for a second, before Midnight tenderly placed his palm on Polly's forehead. Her pale, sunken cheeks flushed pink and she drew in a short, ragged breath. "She's weak, I'm not sure she has the strength left in her for this."

"What did you just do to her?"

"Not all of my talents are dark, Detective Inspector."

The use of his official title was not lost on Gredge.

"I'm aware of that *Mister Gunn*, I was just asking – curiosity if you like."

"Curiosity killed the cat, Inspector."

"Lucky I've got my nine lives intact then, eh? I'm only asking because whatever you did made her look a little better; she's got a bit of colour in her cheeks now."

Midnight removed his hand from Polly's head and turned towards his colleague.

"She has sulphur poisoning from the matches she sells. I just extracted some of the poison from her system that's all. Her cheeks may be flushed but it hasn't helped her much. There's something blocking my ability to heal her and I can't tell what it is."

"You can cure her? Blimey, that'd be something to see. If you could cure the girl she could perhaps give us another eye witness account!"

"If I were to heal her Inspector, it wouldn't be for information. She deserves a second chance at life."

Arthur cleared his throat.

"Well yes, of course. I didn't mean... you know." Pausing, not knowing what else to say for fear of seeming unsympathetic again, Arthur scrubbed a hand over his stubbled chin and tugged at his moustache.

"You don't think she deserves one, Inspector?" Arthur could sense the accusatory tone in the question. He thought carefully about how to answer truthfully without causing offence, but tact was never one of his strong points.

"Of course she deserves one. Every person deserves a good life but that's just it, isn't it? What life does she have? I didn't mean to sound heartless. Christ, I feel terrible for the little wretch but if she could help us catch who did this to her – to all of these poor buggers – it'd give her life some meaning at least. What else has she got? Even if you do cure the girl, are you just going to put her right back on the streets selling matches and dying of sulphur poisoning?"

Midnight's hand went back to the girl's forehead but this time he swept a strand of limp, damp hair away from her delicate face,

"Then I'll find her something else to do," he declared. "Now, shall we get on with what we came here for?"

The Matron had been instructed to clear the room of nurses and not let anyone enter. She had protested loudly, saying she couldn't possibly leave the patients unsupervised but after one glaring look from Midnight she'd backed off.

Midnight was glad Arthur was guarding the door; his dark powers made the Inspector uncomfortable, so it was best he stayed out of the action, but close enough to hear first-hand what he gleaned from the victims.

"They're so weak, it will be hard to tell what's wrong with them. I'm going to try and give them a boost first."

"Like you did with the girl?"

"Like I did with Polly, yes."

He placed his hand on the woman's head and the light glimmered in the ward. The name 'Laura' flashed in his head. The woman's cheeks flushed pink, just as Polly's had, and her breathing eased somewhat. He went from bed to bed sending as much light and healing to each victim as he could manage, but he grew frustrated as he did so; something was still blocking him.

"Damn! There's something in the way. I can't see what it is but if I could move it I could help them."

"You could cure them all?" Arthur's voice rose an octave.

"Not completely; some of them have sustained irreparable organ damage. I can do nothing for that, but I can help with infections and disease. It would extend their lifespan somewhat at least."

Again, Arthur wondered at the point of that. They were all poor souls who looked like they didn't have much of a life to extend. He pondered that it might be more of a blessing to just let them die rather than send them all back to a life of squalor and poverty. Of course, he kept these thoughts to himself. He rather thought, that in this instance, Midnight's respect for life had marred his judgement of what would be a merciful death for some of these poor beggars.

"I'm going to delve into their memories again now, I managed to give them enough strength to cope with it. You can close your eyes if you want to Arthur."

"How did you... ? Oh, never mind, let's just get it done and then we can start finding the sod responsible." Arthur resigned himself to the uncomfortable feeling he knew accompanied the witnessing of Midnight's darker talents and did as his colleague instructed. His lids squeezed shut, his back rigid against the heavy ward door – a bated silence settled over the room.

Midnight opened himself to the darkness, bore the pain of its acceptance with his usual stalwart dignity, and pushed gently into the mind of one of the female victims. As always, with older memories, it was foggy. He had to concentrate hard to make it out.

'Hey Sal! Bring us another pint will ya?'

'Ain't you had enough? I ain't having you pissin' in the corner again 'Arry! Its scares me customers away."

'It ain't the piss what scares 'em Sal, it's the size of me tackle!'

'Away with ya, go on! Dirty bloody bastard.'

"She's a barmaid, her name is Sal."

Arthur jumped at the sound of Midnight's voice and instinctively opened his eyes. He pushed away from the door, suppressing his fears, his detective instincts taking over.

"What else?" Arthur demanded, his notepad already in his hand.

"Wait one moment." Midnight delved again and another memory opened to him.

'Fetch me the bucket Em, quick!'

'You sick again Sal? You don't look so good poppet.'

'I don't feel it neither, I'm dog tired.'

'What's the doc say? Here! Try an aim in the bloody bucket will ya!'

The memory faded in Midnight's mind and another came into view. There was no speech and he could see nothing except for two red glowing orbs surrounded by a black void. Sal's body jerked under his touch, her eyes flew open and her mouth opened in a silent scream. Midnight withdrew from her, her lids closed, and she stilled.

"It's the same as before – red eyes and then nothing. She's very sick too, her liver is damaged. I can't do much for her."

Arthur reached out and patted his colleague's shoulder.

"Well, it's not much to go on but it confirms my suspicions that we're looking at a serial attacker."

Pensive, and momentarily lost in his own thoughts, Midnight moved to the next bed. Here lay a man of around the same age as himself – early to mid-twenties at a guess, although a hard life had aged him somewhat. He was skinny and malnourished with patches of hair missing on his scalp.

"We know this one. His name is Charlie Fenwick, works as a Costermonger round the Docks area. He's pretty well known on account of his unusual selling technique," Arthur said.

"Which is what?" Midnight asked.

"He has quite a profound stutter apparently. I can imagine that's not much cop for a street seller, which is why he sings his wares. The Singing Seller they call him. His sister found him dumped behind some empty barrels dockside. He'd been missing for a week. All we know from his sister is that he told her he had an appointment with someone who was going to help him, and it would change their fortunes. She went looking for him when he didn't come home after two days."

"Let me see what I can find." Midnight reached for the man and after a brief moment he turned to Arthur. "Same. I'm afraid I'm not going to be able to give you much more than I already have."

Arthur shrugged. "No matter, it's more than we had before and enough to give us a few leads to chase up. At least we have names for them all now. Someone's bound to know something. You did me a big favour."

"You'd better let the Matron in. I suspect she's chomping at the bit to find out what we've been doing to her patients."

Arthur scoffed, "I doubt it, she'll be too busy filling in the discharge forms."

"What? Why are they being discharged?"

"Nobody to pay their fees. St. Thomas's isn't a charitable hospital, Midnight. They've been here for weeks whilst under police investigation but their time's up. A couple have families they can go back to and the rest will be transferred to the asylum. The hospital only cares for the sick and wounded not for the mentally afflicted – which is what these poor buggers have been assessed to be."

"What about the girl? Where will they send her?"

Arthur pursed his lips. "I think there's a place for sick orphans over the river somewhere. Don't recall the name."

"I'll pay."

"Eh?"

"Their fees. I'll pay them until something can be worked out, something better than... this." Midnight looked around the crowded, filthy ward in disgust. Arthur shook his head.

"Well, it's your money I suppose. Although I'm not sure where you think you're going to send them that's better than this. It's a warm bed and regular food, probably more than they're used to."

"I'll find something." Midnight's jaw clenched. He was determined to find a solution for these sorry souls. Arthur was right – it was his money and he had lots of it.

3

PLANS

Midnight kept no other staff than his butler, Giles Morgan, and his housekeeper, Clementine Phillips. He liked privacy and efficiency and his two employees offered both. He paid them well and Mrs. Phillips, being an excellent cook, didn't mind the extra duties that would normally fall to cooks and housemaids. The same could be said of Mr. Morgan, who often helped with the hanging out of washing and the dusting of lamps. It was rather unusual in normal polite society, but then again Midnight Gunn went to great lengths not to socialise. He never had visitors or overnight guests, no balls, dinners or card parties. So, it was relatively easy to look after him and his household.

The heavy front door to the mansion groaned loudly as it opened. Midnight kept it that way on purpose; it was easier to hear any unwelcome visitors in the dead of night. Entering the wide hallway, he turned and closed the door behind him, thankful to be home. The entrance hall was lit by a single gas wall lamp by the grand staircase, ensconced in decorative glass and lead-work. Giles must have left it on in readiness for his master's homecoming.

It was past 11pm. He'd finished at Saint Thomas's by the late afternoon, but he'd not gone home afterwards. Needing to clear his mind and shed the remnants of the shadows from his bones, he'd taken a cab and walked around Hyde Park until dark. Then visited a few local pubs and made some polite enquires as to the whereabouts of a missing barmaid named Sal. The locals had been wary of him as usual and his enquiries hadn't turned up much. In truth, he hadn't expected them to; it was just a distraction from thinking about what he'd seen at the hospital.

Now he was home alone and standing in the dim light, the image of the little girl, Polly, came to the forefront of his mind. Her wretched, mutilated body, her pale skin, poisoned blood and her tiny beating heart. Despite all this he had felt a strength in her that was different from the other victims. He'd been able to give her more healing than the rest of them. There'd still been a blockage but he'd felt Polly's shift a little when he had pushed at it. Midnight had thought about that during his time in Hyde Park. Maybe she could be saved, if he paid another visit and pushed a little harder.

Dropping his door key into the ceramic bowl on the hall table, Midnight shrugged off his long black coat, brushing the rain from the shoulders before he hung it on the coat stand.

"Good evening sir. I hope you've had a fruitful day? Might I offer you a hot beverage or a plate of food before you retire?" Giles had appeared through the wood-panelled door to the left of the staircase that led to his quarters. He was dressed in blue striped pyjamas and a heavy, monogrammed velvet dressing gown – a Christmas gift from his employer.

"Good evening Giles, shouldn't you be in bed? I hope you haven't been waiting up for me?" Midnight enquired. The butler replied with a short placatory nod to indicate that he had indeed waited up for his return. "Oh, I am sorry. You really didn't need to, I'm quite capable of fetching myself a drink and a snack of an evening."

"Yes, sir, but I am the butler in this household and I do have certain duties I must attend to."

"Please go to bed and get some rest. I can manage. I'll just pour myself a brandy in the parlour before I retire." Giles didn't move. Midnight sighed, "Fine, I will take a brandy, in the parlour if you please." The butler nodded and padded off in his nightwear and slippers to fetch his master a drink. Midnight walked wearily through the hallway towards the parlour, where the glow from the dying fire served a warm welcome from the cold, wet October evening he'd just come from.

He turned on the gas lights, needing to fill the darkness and chase away the shadows that were always lurking. Today was the first time he'd used his powers on so many people in one day and he felt drained. Kicking off his shoes he flopped down into the leather high-backed chair that faced the fire and warmed his feet. Giles appeared carrying a crystal glass and decanter of brandy on a silver tray. He poured a good inch of the amber liquid into the tumbler and handed it to his master.

"Thank you Giles. Care to join me for one, or are you off to bed?" Mr. Morgan inclined his head and seemed to consider him for a moment before he answered.

"Thank you, sir. Perhaps I might have a small nightcap." He pottered off to fetch another glass and returned shortly with a glass and a bucket of coal.

"Let me do that." Midnight stood and reached for the bucket and was surprised when the butler passed it over. "Pour yourself a brandy and take a seat, I'll soon have us warmed up. It's colder than a witch's wart outside."

"Thank you sir, you are too kind."

"Nonsense. Tonight, we are just two ordinary men sharing a brandy by the fire and airing our woes." Midnight raised his glass towards Giles and the butler reciprocated. He took a large swig then banked up the fire before settling himself back down in the chair. "Ahh, that's better!"

"I take it your Lordship had a troubling day?"

"You could say that, yes." Midnight paused for moment and gazed into the fire, running the edge of the brandy glass over his bottom lip. "I'm rich, Giles."

"Indeed, sir."

"Well what is the use of being rich if you're not going to use it for anything... useful?"

"Does his Lordship have something in mind?"

"Yes. I think I may need your help though."

"I will be happy to assist wherever I may sir. What is it you require?"

"I need a house, Giles. As you know I'm not well acquainted with the city socialites but you and Mrs. Phillips know the staff from the other houses in London, am I correct?"

"A house, sir? Are you not settled in your family home, or is it a country residence you require? Are we about to enter polite society and start entertaining the London gentry? Because if that is the case then you'll be needing to hire quite a few more staff."

"Staff, yes. Entertaining, most certainly not. No Giles, I want to open a hospital for the poor. I need a very large house and lots of staff. It shall be a charitable hospital with myself as benefactor. We'll employ good nurses, and even trained surgeons. I hear there are some incredible advances in medicine these days, Giles. What say you? Will you help me?"

Giles put down his brandy glass and rose from the chair.

He straightened out his dressing gown and sniffed discreetly before looking Midnight in the eye.

"Your father would be very proud." He held out is hand for his employer, who promptly shook it, "As am I, sir."

"Thank you, Giles. That means a lot to me. I take it that is a yes?"

"It would be my honour. I shall send out word first thing in the morning. I must retire now, sir. Thank you for the brandy."

Midnight nodded, smiled and patted Giles' shoulder,

"Goodnight, Giles. Sleep well." As the butler retreated from the parlour Midnight called out, "We need a *big* house! Not too far out of the city but with clean air!"

"Of course your Lordship." came a faint reply from the hallway.

"And have Mrs. Phillips begin interviews for staff! We'll need nurses and surgeons!"

"Indeed, sir. I shall inform Mrs. Phillips in the morning," came Giles' barely audible reply. Midnight grinned; he didn't need his butler's approval to spend his own money, but he found he wanted it all the same. Giles had been the closest thing he'd had to a paternal figure since his own father, Josiah, had died ten winters ago from a massive heart attack. Midnight flopped happily back in to his chair and took up the brandy glass once more, swigging the remaining liquid down in one gulp. He smiled and shook his head. He'd been invited to work on several cases in the past with Scotland Yard, he'd wandered the filth-ridden streets of London many times, given alms to the poor and healed the needy, but had never felt inspired to embark on such a large and very public venture before. Midnight preferred to stay out of the public eye, never attending balls or dinners – despite sometimes being invited. He wondered what had changed in the last twenty-four hours. The pale and innocent face of little Polly appeared in his mind again. He blinked it away and ran a hand over his face. No, it wasn't the girl, she was just another poor orphan on the street. *One you could help,* his conscience reminded him. That part at least was correct; he could help her, he had felt it. Midnight was convinced that if he went to her again, he could fix her.

He felt his weary eyes start to close as he gazed into the dancing flames in the hearth. Too exhausted to make his way up the long winding staircase to his bed, he slouched in the high-backed chair and allowed sleep to take him. Little Polly's face followed him to his dreams.

4

SPRING-HEELED JACK

Perched atop a roof overlooking the narrow alley, he waited. Lit only by the muted glow from the tavern's filthy window, the alley provided the perfect opportunity to locate his next target. The faint light below barely reached a few feet beyond the ale house entrance, ensuring his complete concealment. The incessant rain pounded down. Cold, wet rivulets trickled past the upturned collar of his black cloak, but he didn't care. The rain concealed his presence as much as the darkness. It muffled his steps as he clambered across the slate-tiled roof and shimmied down the drainpipe. His steel claws scraped along the metal during the descent but the sound was swallowed by shadows and the gushing water that poured from the gutter.

A woman had exited the tavern, alone and clearly inebriated. It was her. His heart rate increased, beating a rapid rhythm in his ears which excited him. He allowed her a few moments' head start; mostly to ensure nobody followed her from the pub. Then, he began the hunt.

Rainwater sloshed along the gullies of the cobbled streets and over his leather boots. It seeped through the fabric of his heavy cloak but he didn't feel it – the blood galloping through his veins kept out the cold. The woman ahead of him staggered suddenly. Throwing her arm sideways, she steadied herself against the brick wall. Upon rising, her head tilted slightly when the sharp clip of his heeled boots behind her caught a cobblestone and resonated loudly through the dimly lit alley. She'd heard him. He cursed inwardly. He did not want the hunt to end just yet. He needed to build the chase and heighten her fear gradually, otherwise it wouldn't work.

The woman quickened her step and he followed quietly. He needed everything to be perfect. The timing had to be just right. Pulling his collar tighter around his neck to hide his face, he focused on his sordid game of cat and mouse.

It was working. The effects of the alcohol she'd consumed were being burned away by her increasing sense of imminent danger. His subtle noises, footfalls and soft humming had gradually alerted her to his presence and he could tell she had begun to panic. Her sense of self-preservation had kicked in but coupled with the alcohol, rain and darkness, she'd become confused and lost. Small whimpers escaped her; any moment now she would run. He readied himself: This was it, the final part of the hunt, the part he was most looking forward to.

"Help me!" she screamed, beginning to run as fast as her skirts would allow. He didn't panic but jogged along as a steady pace behind her. She'd run down a commercial back alley, there were no residents to call on for aid. She was trapped.

"There, there, pretty one," he soothed. "No need to shout, no one to hear you. Just me and you my sweet." The menacing undertones in his inflection excited him – he knew what was coming. She'd backed herself up against a wall, head turning frantically back and forth – looking for an escape. He slowed his advance, scraping his metal claws along the brick. The sound made her shrink further into herself, as if she was trying to fade into the wall behind her. Wanting the anticipation to build and feed her fear, he began a soft hum and lowered his collar.

"Your eyes!" she cried as the red glow fell upon her face. "What are you?"

"I am the devil come to claim your soul, pretty." The phrase dripped salaciously from his tongue and her reaction thrilled him.

"No! Please, please sir. I'm begging you, don't kill me! Help me! Somebody, help!"

He reached her and pinned her mouth shut with his hand. The cold metal claws dug into her cheek and she went rigid. Eyes wide like a frightened rabbit, she breathed rapidly through her nostrils. He pressed himself against her, pinning her tight against the wall, and stared directly into her eyes. She had nowhere to run, he had her under his complete control. He was surprised to find himself aroused. That hadn't happened on the previous hunts, even the time with the well-to-do woman. Although her death had been an accident. He hadn't meant to kill, merely to harvest. Perhaps that was what lay at the back of his mind now. He had no plans to kill, but his physical reaction to this woman's fear couldn't be denied. The thought of a kill aroused him. His hand slipped from her mouth during his moment of distraction.

"Take me then, just don't kill me please. I have a child. Please, I'll do anything."

He didn't understand at first what she was saying but when she moved her hips towards him, her upper thigh brushed his hardness. He almost laughed, she thought he wanted to rape her! He opened his mouth to tell her she was a disgusting whore for offering herself so easily but a thought occurred to him: maybe he could use this to his advantage.

"Dirty little bitch! This is what you want isn't it?" He leered, trailing a single cold claw down her cheek and neck towards her chest, piercing her breast. The woman cried out and blood began to trickle from the cut, staining the top of her chemise.

"Don't 'urt me! Please?" She cried.

He clamped her mouth shut again and with his other hand, slashed her chemise open to reveal a bare, blood covered breast. Her eyes bulged with fear as he bent his head, extended his blackened tongue and lapped greedily at the trickle of blood. When he reached her exposed nipple, he took it in his mouth and bit down hard. The woman screamed into his hand and struggled against him. He kept her in his mouth and moved his free hand to hitch up her skirts. Her muffled screams encouraged him when the sharp steeply points of his hand gouged raw, bloody trails into her thigh.

It was working. He could sense it coming. That glorious moment was almost upon him. The time for capture was near.

"Oi! You there!" Came a distant shout. "Who goes there?" The voice was a little closer this time and accompanied by footsteps. The sudden interruption caused him to jerk away from the woman and twist back to see who was advancing. He saw a figure striding quickly towards them, silhouetted against the light from the single glass lamp at the end of the street. He recognised the outline as a member of the constabulary. Damn! How frustrating! Just as he was at the moment of capture too.

His distracted state caused him to momentarily lose his concentration and then he felt a shove, followed by excruciating pain in his groin. He felt the pain spread to his abdomen and he struggled not to vomit. The woman had kicked him right between his legs!

"Copper! 'Ere help me! He tried to kill me!" she yelled and

ran towards her rescuer, bare tit bouncing and bleeding, and her clothes in tatters. The bobby quickened pace and, raising his truncheon, he blew hard on his whistle in three long blasts.

"Stop! Stop right there! You're under arrest!" The bobby shouted but the creature-like figure, struggling to stand upright after the assault on his crotch, catapulted himself ten-feet into the air and disappeared over the brick wall into the night. "What the bleeding 'ell?" The constable stood stock still, mouth agog, as the wailing woman flung herself into his body and clung to him.

"Thank 'eavens you came sir! I thought I was a goner, I did! It tried to... to... Oh, gawd sir, the things he was doing." She broke down and he gently laid a protective arm around her shoulders.

"Now then young lady, you're safe now. We need to get you home, I'll take a statement when we get there. Where do you live?"

"It's not far sir, walking distance I reckon... I got lost when that thing was chasing me."

"Well, cover yourself up miss and let's get off then." He noticed the blood and wound on her chest and gestured towards her, "You need a doctor?"

The young woman blushed as she attempted to arrange the rags of her chemise to cover her bare breast and the Constable politely averted his gaze.

"It's Bessie. My name's Bessie. Ain't got no money to pay for a doctor. My sister is at home with the baby, she'll fix me up."

They set off walking and a moment later the Constable stopped.

"What did you mean when you called him a 'thing'?" he

asked, his brows creased. Bessie, still pale as a sheet and visibly shaken, replied

"It weren't no human. No chance. Never seen nothing like it I ain't. Its eyes glowed blood red and he had 'orrible claws! You saw what it did? No human could jump over a wall like that." Bessie shuddered and wrapped her arms around herself, hunkering her shoulders. "T'ain't natural. Like he had ruddy springs in his heels."

5

READ ALL ABOUT IT

Giles placed the breakfast tray, containing two letters and the morning newspaper - neatly folded of course - on the table next to Midnight.

"Ah! Thank you, Giles. I hope these letters are what I think they are!" He glanced at the butler who gave a brief nod and smiled.

"Would sir like bacon or salmon with his eggs this morning?"

"Both please."

Giles's left eyebrow arched in response to the odd combination of salty pork *and* smoked fish but served it up on the plate nevertheless.

"Yes!" Midnight leapt out of his chair, fist in the air, causing Giles to startle and drop the plate of food he was carrying. "Oh! Giles, did I do that? I am sorry." He dropped the letter he'd been reading and quickly bent to help his butler clean up the mess on the floor.

"No need, I can manage." Giles tried to keep the chastising tone from his voice but didn't succeed. Midnight chuckled.

"You sounded just like my father then," he beamed. "Come

now, let me help? It was my fault after all." The old butler sighed and resigned himself to being helped by his master but not before Midnight caught the merest glimpse of a smile. He was sure the comparison to his father was the cause. Since the untimely death of Josiah Gunn, Giles had taken over complete care of the then almost sixteen-year-old Midnight. Having no other family that he knew of – none had attended his father's funeral – Midnight had relied solely on Giles and the remaining household staff during his transition into adult-hood. He trusted Giles entirely, as his father had. Josiah had never remarried after his mother, Josephine, had died giving birth to him. There were paintings of his mother all over the Gunn mansion and her bedroom had been left as it was before her passing. Nothing had been removed, sold or given away. The whole house was a shrine to his mother. Josiah had relied heavily on the company of his butler. All social events and gatherings had stopped and Josiah's presence in polite society had gradually faded. Midnight had never known a banquet to be held at their home and nobody had ever made social calls. His father only ever dealt with businessmen and colleagues. He'd thrown himself into making money, and he'd been good at it, trebling the family fortunes in the fifteen years following his beloved wife's death. Midnight imagined that Giles and Josiah must have become more than employer and employee during that time, they'd become friends of a sort. Giles was the only constant presence in the house and thus became his father's confidant. Upon Josiah's passing, it was Giles that guided the young Midnight in the business affairs of his father and so it followed that Midnight carried forth the same rela-tionship. He trusted Giles with his life.

When the mash up of eggs, bacon and salmon had been scraped from the rug, Midnight wiped his hands on the napkin and reached for the letter.

"Read it!" he exclaimed, a huge broad grin spread across his chiselled face. Giles took the letter and began to read. A few moments later, he passed it back with an approving nod.

"Excellent news, sir. When are you planning on a visit?"

"No time like the present I'd say. What say you Giles, fancy a day trip?"

"Me?" The butler looked a little taken aback. Midnight clapped him on the shoulder,

"Of course man! Who else would I trust to give me sound advice? Get your coat and I'll ready a cab."

Giles spluttered, "But the breakfast!"

"Breakfast is over and this cannot wait. We must pounce before anyone else seizes the opportunity!" Midnight noticed the dilemma on his butler's face – he was looking at the rug and frowning. "You're worrying about the smell, aren't you?"

"Smoked salmon will leave terrible stench, sir!"

"I'll inform Mrs. Phillips, I'm sure she'll have some wondrous concoction that will bring it right out. Now, go and fetch your coat and hat and let's enjoy a jolly!"

WHEN THEY WERE SETTLED in the cab, en route to the address, Giles handed Midnight the morning paper that he'd brought from the breakfast table.

"Something you may want to look at, sir."

Midnight was intrigued and unfolded the paper on his lap. The headline on the front page of the *Morning Post* read:

Spring-Heeled Jack
Murderous Villain Terrorises London!

A spate of terrible attacks upon the helpless city residents is causing wide-spread panic. The attacks, spread over the course of

*the last two months or more, have been perpetrated by a
frightening creature not of this world. Our sources say that a
mysterious demon-like creature, which takes human form, has
been responsible for the murder of at least one victim: Miss
Emeline Rowbotham, the daughter of wealthy merchant, Robert
Rowbotham. It has been indicated that the number of attacks is
vast and have been concentrated around the Southwark area.
Scotland Yard, leading the investigation, have refused to comment
but want to ensure city residents that there is no need to panic and
to go about their daily business. Any suspicious activity should be
reported to a local police station.*

*Latest victim and lucky survivor Bessie Green said in her
statement to the press:*

*"It was inhuman, a vicious monster with claws, 8ft tall and
black as the night, like a giant bat!"*

*Miss Green said the black-tongued, red-eyed creature escaped
by leaping over a 10ft brick wall when she was rescued by
Constable Henry Perch. Constable Perch corroborated Miss
Green's story of the creature's spectacular and impossible escape.*

The story continued and was accompanied by a detailed
sketch of a monstrous figure leaping over a wall. Midnight
slammed the paper down on the cab seat and swore.

"Blasted reporters! Gredge assured me this wouldn't go
public. That's all we need is to set the whole of bloody London
on edge. There'll be a ton of false reports flooding in from the
panicked public now – jumping at shadows and alley cats!" He
thumped a fisted hand against the cab wall and swore again.

"I take it you have no further clues as to the situation then
sir?" asked Giles.

"Nothing gets past you does it?"

The butler inclined his head.

"A quick glance at the article this morning whilst setting

the breakfast tray, coupled with your recent nightly activities merely raised my suspicions, sir. I can usually tell when you're involved with an investigation."

"You can?"

"Indeed, sir. You become...agitated and overzealous."

The corner of Midnight's mouth twitched a little.

"Overzealous? How so?"

The butler looked out of the small window as the cab jostled to and fro, the horses' hooves clopping along at a steady pace on the cobbles.

"Current destination: a warehouse at the docks with a view to converting it into a charitable hospital for the poor and needy." Giles stated dryly.

"A project of which you approved if I'm not mistaken?"

"Indeed sir, indeed. However, I do recall suggesting several suitable small country houses that needed little intervention to enable the project. You chose a near derelict warehouse."

"Yes but those houses were outside the city; what use is that to the people of London? I'm grateful of course, Giles, for your efforts, but that warehouse is perfect! It's cheaper than the houses, it has a huge amount of space. I mean just imagine the number of patients we could fit in there! It has a great deal of potential don't you think? I have such plans Giles! There's space enough for in-house nurses' quarters, separate wards. It's right by the docks, exactly where it's needed the most."

Giles was grinning and shaking his head in a placatory way. Midnight stopped mid-speech, mouth hanging open like a fish, and then he conceded with a grin of his own.

"Overzealous...but admirably so sir," Giles said smiling. "I hope you catch him soon," he added, nodding towards the crumpled newspaper. Midnight sighed heavily and turned his face towards the window to gaze out.

"I have to," he said simply. "I just have to." He thought of little Polly, sick as she was, being sent to God-knows-where and having no effective treatment or care. She'd be hidden away in some desolate room in a rundown orphanage. She wouldn't last long in her frail state. He thought of the others, even the ones lucky enough to have families to help care for them. All they could do really was wait for them to die. The poor had no access to medical care or useful medicines if they couldn't pay for them. Yes, he had to do something fast. He had to catch this creature and stop it and he had to do something to help the poor people of his beloved city. Even if he was having trouble finding any useful leads on the killer, he felt that pursuing the hospital project was somewhat productive in getting those victims out of harm's way and starting to fight back against the ills of such a class-divided society.

It was true, he'd been born into privilege but that didn't mean he couldn't use his wealth for the benefit of those who needed it more. Truth be known he'd never felt at home among polite society. The seedy public houses, raucous music halls and open parks of London had proved more appealing, the people more real. What some might consider the dregs of society, Midnight thought of as the heart of the city. A city with no heart was just an empty shell, a facade.

Sometime later the hansom rattled to a stop and Giles exited first to hold the door open for his master. He paid the cabby and gave a generous tip, then the unlikely pair proceeded to the address in the letter. Midnight, dressed in the best that Savile Row tailoring could offer, appeared every inch the perfect aristocrat. Nobody passing him in the street would guess what unnatural power lurked beneath the fine clothes, top hat and confident walk. He could blend in if he had a mind to. However, if one got too close one might sense there was more to the man than first appeared. Midnight was careful not to bump into anyone on the busy street; sometimes if this happened, he inadvertently caught a glimpse of a memory or was flooded by strong emotions emanating from passers-by. Useful in certain circumstances, but today he needed a clear mind.

They halted their steps outside a large run-down warehouse a little way from the dockyards. The frontage was quite spectacular for a commercial establishment. A large arched double doorway faced the Thames in the centre of the brick building and two long arched windows stood guard either side of the entrance, adding to its grandeur. Midnight looked towards the roof as he examined the outer perimeter and laughed when he noticed it adorned with gruesome gargoyles. These quirky architectural features gave the warehouse an almost ecclesiastical feel, something Midnight found quite ironic and vastly amusing.

"I think this might just do, Giles. What say you?"

"I would say let us examine the interior before making any rash decisions sir."

"Of course, you're right. But don't you feel it?"

"Feel it, sir?"

"It's alive Giles – a sleeping giant just waiting to awaken to its true purpose," he pointed upwards to the gargoyles, "see there? Gargoyles are protectors, they keep away bad spirits. Now, I ask you, why would gargoyles be atop a warehouse?"

"One would assume, to keep the contents of said warehouse safe, sir." Giles replied.

"Oh yes, no doubt. *But*, their true purpose is to protect the people that will be attending our little hospital!"

"If you say so." Said Giles indulgently.

"I feel it, its heart has quickened pace. It calls to me. Let's go inside."

The auctioneer met them at the door and let them in. As they entered, light streaked across the dimly lit floor, the movement threw up dust particles that danced merrily in the sunbeams – their welcoming committee. Midnight reached out his hand to them and drank in the warmth. Pleasant, calm sensations washed over him, reaffirming his opinion that they had found the perfect location for the hospital. The auctioneer was prattling on, delivering his rehearsed sales patter, when Midnight interrupted.

"When is the auction?"

"Two days hence sir, there's been much interest in this building. I hear the East India Company have shown a liking for it." Midnight knew this was not good news; the East India Company virtually ran London's commercial import and export trade. He would be going up against some of London's wealthiest Barons. No matter, he decided, one way or another he would hold the deeds to this wonderful property. He would use whatever methods – or powers – were needed to attain it.

6

A LEAD

"Listen, I know what you're saying Midnight, but I need leads. Leaking that story to the press might just throw up some new information. I know we'll have a hundred and one false reports to sift through, but it's worth it if just one of them can give us a lead."

"A hundred and one false reports and possible widespread panic." Midnight interjected. "But yes, I suppose I understand your logic, Arthur." He took a sip of his tea and sat forward in his chair. The small tea rooms overlooked St James' Park. Arthur had requested an urgent meeting with him to discuss the progress on the Spring-Heeled Jack case, of which there turned out to be little. "What happens now?" He looked at his pocket watch briefly. He had about twenty minutes left before he had to be at the auction house.

"I need your help with something," said Arthur.

"Go on."

"Right, here's what we know so far." Gredge got out his notebook and pencil and ran through a roughly scrawled list, "All but one of the victims were local to Southwark, all but one survived, all victims were suffering in some way before their attack, and a couple of 'em had spoken of some kind of meeting or appointment before they disappeared." Gredge ticked each item on the list as he read. "That's the victims. The killer is described as unusually tall," he snorted dismissively remembering Bessie Green's description of her 8ft tall attacker, "red, glowing eyes, metal claws and a black tongue." Gredge put his notepad down on the table and took a gulp of his cooling tea. "Seems to me there's not much to go on in terms of clues but the one thing that stands out to me is the rich girl. She doesn't fit."

Midnight considered this and agreed.

"So, we go back and talk to the Rowbothams again?"

Arthur nodded, "Seems the only thing we can do at present. I'm sure I'm missing something there. I got the feeling the family weren't being entirely truthful when we last spoke."

"Rowbotham's it is then. Only not today; I have a rather important auction to attend and I'm running late." Midnight glanced again at his pocket watch. He rose from his seat and began putting on his hat. Gredge rose too.

"Auction? You buying land or property?"

"I'm buying a solution, Arthur. Or a beginning. Either way I'm running late. Feel free to accompany me if you wish. I'm meeting Giles at the auction house in five minutes, we can continue our chat on the way."

"Yes, alright. I will, I'm intrigued." Arthur smirked. His curious mind had gotten the better of him. If truth be known he wanted to be nosey and find out more about the mysterious Midnight Gunn. Over the years, he had come to think of him as a friend as well as a colleague. They had met in unusual circumstances five years ago, during the case of the Peckham vampire (which had turned out to be nothing more than a man with a fetish for drinking blood). They had continued to work together, when necessary, ever since. But Arthur knew little of Midnight's personal business aside from his residential address which he'd sometimes visited in a professional capacity. They'd never socialised outside of police matters. He found now that he couldn't refuse the opportunity to witness a possible business transaction and was curious to know of this 'solution' his friend spoke of and its purpose.

THE AUCTION HOUSE was jam-packed with London's finest, all dressed in their most business-like garb. Over-fed, red-faced gentry jostled for prime position in the room, greeting each other in loud, blustering voices, plastering on their friendliest smiles but secretly planning to steal prize properties from under each other's noses. Midnight hated it. He could never envisage a time where he might willingly enter such social circles. He was reluctant when business matters required him to mingle with his so-called peers. Still, today warranted the effort it took to nod, smile and greet politely those who approached him. Some recognised him from previous transactions, legal or financial matters, and some were merely curious to know who the dapper young man accompanied by a detective and a butler was. Midnight bore it the best he could and was thankful when the auctioneer rapped his gavel on the wooden podium to indicate the start of the day's business.

The warehouse was fourth in the catalogue. Midnight noticed the heavies from the East India Trading Company sit to attention. This was it. He gathered his thoughts and readied his armoury. He glanced at Arthur to his left who, up till now, had looked decidedly bored. but recognising the apprehension of Gunn's face leaned forward eagerly. Midnight then looked to his right; Giles adjusted his cravat and bowler, preparing himself for the battle ahead. He gave his friend and master an approving nod and then the auction began.

Twenty minutes later the tension in the room was palpable, three bidders competed for the win. Midnight kept his cool, not even glancing in his competitors' direction. After two more rounds the third bidder dropped out leaving him and the big wigs from the East India Company. This is when things got serious – nobody went head to head with East India for long. This group of men represented the wealth of the whole of London; they owned, ran, or had stock in almost every large import and export business in the city. It did not do well to challenge their status quo but Midnight did not scare easily. Neither did he have limitless amounts of money; his coffers were full to brimming but they were nothing compared to the seemingly infinite collective wealth of his opponents. He did not favour underhanded tactics but sometimes the cause outweighed the method and the people of London needed this. Polly needed this. In this particular circumstance cheating was necessary.

Midnight let the bidding continue for another few rounds until the price rose high enough for it not to be too suspicious when his opponents gave up the ghost. He raised his hand and put in his own bid, and then he slowly began to call on the shadows. Nobody but Giles and Gredge noticed the room grow increasingly dim.

"What are you doing?" Gredge hissed.

"Winning," Midnight said simply. The big wigs conspiratorial mutterings quickly turned to arguments among their group. The bloated toads rowing over the prize lily-pad began to draw the attention of the whole room and the auctioneer, whilst Midnight sat calmly and waited. The gavel banged loudly several times as the auctioneer called for order.

"I say! Order! The bid lies with this gentleman in the left

corner," the auctioneer declared, gesturing to where Midnight sat, "Order! I must ask if any of you intend to bid further, gentlemen, please!" He banged his gavel so hard Midnight was surprised it didn't break. The auctioneer was so flustered his face was almost purple. Meanwhile the respected gentry from the East India Trading Company were almost to fisticuffs, it seemed none of them could agree whether to continue bidding or not. Other patrons had become involved, attempting to calm the situation down. Most just looked appalled or confused at the ungentlemanly outburst and were chuffing and muttering their disgust to their neighbours.

Arthur Gredge stared in total wonderment at the scene that played out in front of him. The auctioneer had had enough and slammed his gavel down one last time before yelling as loudly as he could,

"Sold! To the gentleman in the corner!"

Midnight nodded and a smile spread across his face. Rising from his seat, Giles congratulated him.

"Well done sir! A most entertaining battle and you emerged victorious." he shook Midnight's hand vigorously then added dryly, "Who would've thought it?"

"Thank you Giles. The outcome is most pleasing indeed!"

He turned to face Arthur who stood with both hands on his hips shaking his head as though he could not believe what he'd just witnessed.

"You cheated," he whispered.

"Are you going to arrest me Arthur?"

"I ought to."

"But you're not." It was not a question.

"No. I'm not. I'll never work you out Midnight but I know you must have a bloody good reason for doing whatever it is you just did."

"The best reason." Midnight assured him.

"Well, I can't say it didn't please me to see them lot lose out for once." Arthur indicated towards the group of now baffled-looking men, "How about you tell me over a pint? No tea – a pint and the truth."

"I am rather parched, Arthur. Auctions seem to make one's thirst insatiable!" He grinned and slapped him on the arm. "Giles, will you join us?"

"Alas sir, much as it would thrill me to accompany you for a 'pint', somebody must attend to daily chores and Mrs. Philips cannot do it alone."

"Ever the professional, Giles." Midnight sighed. "Thank you for attending today. Please inform the ever-lovely Clementine, I shall be home for dinner at six-thirty sharp." Giles nodded and left, leaving midnight and Arthur to wander off to the nearest pub for an ale. As they walked and chatted side by side, Midnight couldn't help but notice that the day seemed a little brighter and his step a little lighter than before.

7

TRUTH AND LIES

The Rowbotham's home was grand but gaudy. The family was not from traditional landed gentry but were what people referred to as 'new money' and some would declare their taste in decor as vulgar. Midnight cared not a jot how people chose to decorate their houses, grand mansion or slum made no difference to him. A family that grieved for their lost daughter sat before him and grief is a great equaliser. He, of course could sympathise with their pain and he could tell that it was heartfelt and genuine. He could also tell that they were holding back. Midnight could sense emotions and he could feel the lies rolling off Mr. Rowbotham's tongue.

"She was a sensible girl. She favoured the music halls but only when accompanied by myself and her mother. She would never willingly go there alone."

"And you have no idea why your daughter would be in that area on a Saturday evening if it wasn't to visit a show?" Gredge enquired.

"None. None at all." Mr. Rowbotham shifted in his seat.

"What about this appointment? Last we spoke, you said

she had arranged to meet somebody. Have you remembered who?"

Mrs. Rowbotham cleared her throat, which earned her a cautionary look from her husband. Midnight leaned forward in his chair and spoke calmly and directly to her.

"Your daughter, it seems, was a fine young lady. About to enter the prime of her life, the world at her feet. What a dreadful waste it would be if her murderer remained at large. I can assure you Mrs. Rowbotham, what passes between us in this room is entirely confidential. Arthur and I," – he hoped the use of first names would put her at ease – "we just want to catch the culprit and see him punished for what he did to poor Miss Emeline." Midnight saw Mrs. Rowbotham's face twitch as if she were fighting back tears. He continued his plea; changing tactics he said, "There are others. Alive, but very much suffering by his hands. A young child named Polly. She's around seven years old, a pitiful scrap of a girl. It's too late to save your Emeline Mrs. Rowbotham, but you can help Polly. We just need more information, anything..."

"Nightingale!" Mrs. Rowbotham blurted out, unable to hold in her grief any longer, "Somebody called Nightingale. She... Emeline, she had trouble. Anxiety, if you will. She had trouble coping with the demands of a young woman in polite society."

"Dearest, please..." Her husband laid a hand on hers.

"No. It needs to be said my love. We must bear the shame, it is our fault. We are the ones who thrust her into the limelight, into a world she didn't belong." She patted her husband's hand, dabbed her eyes with a kerchief and continued. "We made enquiries with the doctors in Harley Street to see if anyone could help her. Her mind was unsettled. They gave her medicine to calm her nerves and it worked for a time. But then she needed more and more, and the doctors wouldn't prescribe it. She began to seek it elsewhere. At first, she paid one of the servants to acquire it. We found out and had to terminate our footman's employment. Then she would take trips out of the house, unaccompanied, and sometimes not come back for hours, but when she did she was always happy and calm. She would sleep for a long time, and we thought she was perhaps getting better. She started sneaking out after dinner in the evenings and when we challenged her about it she said she'd found a Nightingale – an angel in disguise who was helping her. She seemed so happy we... we should've stopped her... Oh! What have we done? It's all our fault!" Mrs. Rowbotham broke down in tears, her husband tried to comfort her.

"So it was this Nightingale she had planned to meet the night she disappeared?" Gredge asked. Mr. Rowbotham nodded.

"Yes but I'm afraid that's all we know, except that he resides in Southwark somewhere. We've searched her room and her belongings for a calling card or anything that might tell us who they are. My wife thinks this Nightingale may be able to tell us something, anything that may put our minds at peace."

"Information that would've been useful to us at the time of initial investigation." Gredge said under his breath. Midnight shot him a look and Gredge shrugged.

"Do you perhaps have any of Miss Emeline's medicine left?" Midnight asked.

"Yes, it's in her room. I'll go and fetch it." Mrs. Rowbotham got up, straightened her skirts and left the room. Mr. Rowbotham looked uncomfortable.

"You understand," he appealed directly to Midnight, "being a gentleman of ... new social standing is very hard. One must fight for one's place in polite society, prove oneself both in business and in one's personal affairs. In my precarious position, I... I cannot afford a scandal." He didn't say any more but looked down at his hands.

"Indeed," Midnight replied. He didn't trust himself to elaborate. How cruel this world was that a person and his family could be so petrified of ruin because of their daughter's struggles. He thought again of the bulbous old toads at the auction and felt even more justified in his actions against them. They were landed gentry like himself but they were worlds apart, still stuck in the trappings of aristocratic etiquette, getting fat on other people's toils and strife. Mayhap he should tell Mr. Rowbotham not to aim too high for he wouldn't like the company he would be keeping. But the loss of their only daughter amid fear of social ruin, was probably indication enough.

Mrs. Rowbotham returned with a small wooden box. Arthur took it and examined the engravings on the exterior. He opened it and sniffed the contents.

"Opium," he stated and passed it to Midnight who also sniffed and nodded in agreement. The wooden box was adorned with curious carvings, Chinese in origin. One in particular caught Midnight's eye – a tiny double-headed dragon, engraved in the bottom right corner. It was separate from the rest of the design, lost like an insignia of sorts,

"Arthur, look here. Does this look familiar?" Arthur bent to look and shook his head.

"Not particularly. What are you thinking?"

"It doesn't fit with the rest of the design, I think it's a mark or a badge, perhaps some club or gang symbol?"

"Hmm, you could be right. It's worth a look." Arthur turned to the Rowbotham's. "May we borrow this for a time?"

"If you think it'll help." Mr. Rowbotham shrugged despondently.

"Thank you. Well, I think we have made some progress today. I'll be in touch. I apologise for the intrusion."

Midnight stood up, shook Mr. Rowbotham's hand and kissed the hand of his wife.

"I'm sorry for your loss, I truly am, and I promise we will find whoever did this to your daughter."

Gunn followed Arthur out of the door and on to the street. Gredge turned to Midnight waving the little wooden box in front of him.

"I bloody knew they were hiding something! Never expected an opium addicted daughter though. At least we have a line of investigation now."

"I take it you'll be hitting the opium dens next then?"

"You yes, me no. They'll smell a copper a mile off. If you'd oblige me, that is?"

Midnight wanted nothing more than to put an end to these attacks and catch the fiend that had killed Emeline Rowbotham and hurt little Polly and the others. The contrast between the Midnight that helped Scotland Yard and the reluctant aristocrat that managed his father's estate was vast. Although fortunate enough to have money, land and title, he preferred not to sit idle. His wealth merely reminded him that he had much more than others. He was generous with his fortune; always making donations to worthy causes that supported London's poor. He would often frequent the poorest boroughs in the evening, using the shadows to mask his presence. That way he found he could observe in inconspicuous anonymity. What he witnessed there appealed to his conscience and fuelled his desire to help wherever he could. Something about solving crimes made him feel alive, useful... normal. Midnight agreed to Gredge's request, much to the relief of the Inspector who nodded back and strode off to hail them a cab.

Polly's tiny pale face haunted Midnight. He didn't know why, but that tiny scrap of a child had gotten under his skin. He'd seen many children in dire straits in need of food, warmth and shelter and he'd helped indirectly with hefty donations to orphanages and hospitals, but had never before allowed himself to become emotionally involved. What made Polly different? He decided it was time for another visit to St. Thomas'. Perhaps this time he could help her, maybe help them all.

8

RESCUE

"Polly the match girl, Sal the barmaid, Charlie Fenwick who worked as a costermonger, Billy Bromley from the rope yard and Laura Carter, she worked down at the White Hart and lived in Southwark with her Mum and two sisters. Those are the only ones left." Gredge ticked names off his list and shook his head. "What a bloody waste."

"Of lives or of potential leads?"

"Bloody hell Gunn, I'm not totally unsympathetic you know. Of course I mean a waste of life... although you have to admit, it's a damn shame you never got another stab at getting some information out of the others before they popped their clogs." Arthur sighed and blew air out of his pursed lips. "Now we just need to chase up this bunch and see if the families will allow us access... if they aren't dead already." He added.

"May I see?" Arthur handed Midnight a few documents. They were standing in the outer corridor of the ward at St Thomas' with the discharge papers the Matron had given Gredge. Two of the female patients had passed away since their last visit and the remaining victims were either with

family or being 'left to rot', as Midnight saw it, in various insti-
tutions for the mentally disturbed.

"Carter and Fenwick have gone home to family, lucky they
had someone to claim them really. Bromley, Sal and the girl
have gone to the All Souls Asylum."

"Polly is in an asylum?" Midnight grabbed the remaining
documents from Arthur and studied them, frowning. "I
thought she was going to an orphanage?"

"Well, one would assume nobody would want to adopt a
virtual corpse," said Arthur dryly.

"We're going there, now!" Midnight thrust the papers back
at Arthur and strode off at a determined pace down the corridor. Arthur followed,

"I suppose we are."

As THE CARRIAGE pulled up outside, Midnight craned his head
out of the window and was met with a terrible sense of foreboding. The battered sign out front read *All Souls Pauper
Asylum* in black with bronze lettering. The huge iron entrance
gate stood tall and grim amid a great brick wall that
surrounded the property.

The two colleagues alighted from the carriage and
Midnight gave the cabbie instructions to wait there for their
return. The rusting iron gate creaked loudly as it swung labo-
riously open, allowing them to enter. They walked up a
sweeping dirt driveway towards the front door of a once grand-
looking house, which now stood in a sorry state of disrepair
and neglect. Midnight could tell immediately that this establishment was vastly underfunded, running on bare-boned
charity from however many benefactors they could muster
sympathies from for the poor people of London. His stride

lengthened. His determination to get to Polly and the others as fast as he could was foremost in his mind. Arthur had to jog to keep up with him.

"Slow down! What's the rush? It's not as if they're going anywhere is it?"

"This isn't right. I need to see them, now!"

Midnight rapped hard on the wooden entrance and the door opened to a smiling woman in her mid-forties, dressed in plain black with white apron and cap. Strands of wispy greying hair stuck out randomly from under her cap and her cheeks were slightly flushed, giving her a flustered appearance.

"Can I help you gentlemen?"

Arthur stepped forward, "Detective Inspector Gredge of Scotland Yard, Ma'am, we're here to see three of your patients."

"Oh. I see. I suppose you'd better come in then." She stood to the side to let them in. "Which patients are you wanting then? Only we're 'avin a skit in the common room see and I'd hate to disturb 'em. Poor beggars don't get much entertaining."

Midnight was first through the door. He looked around briefly as if deciding which way to go as Arthur spoke to the attendant.

"We need to see a young amputee by the name of Polly, a woman of around twenty years old called Sal and an older gent; Billy Bromley. They were all transfers from St Thomas' earlier this week."

The woman nodded.

"Ah yes, I remember. Mr. Bromley and Miss Sally, that's what we call her, are upstairs in their rooms and the little Miss is in the parlour there enjoying the skit."

Midnight didn't hesitate, he headed straight for the parlour in the direction the woman had pointed.

"I suppose I'll be going upstairs then?" Arthur shouted after him, but he got no reply. He indicated to the woman, whose name was Annie, to show him upstairs and left Midnight to find Polly.

The parlour was quite sizeable and light for a property of this type. Four arched windows ran the length of the back wall opposite the door and rows of chairs had been placed in front of a makeshift stage where a magic show was taking place. The performer was dressed in black and white striped trousers and bright red coat tails, his face was painted white but for the two black vertical lines over his eyes and a red painted nose, his black moustache and beard a stark contrast to the white paint.

The magician momentarily halted his performance as Midnight burst into the room and began scanning the rows of chairs. The performer scowled at the interruption and began an exaggerated mime for his audience, chastising the intruder. He waged a gloved finger in Midnight's direction and mimicked giving him a good spanking. The actions prompted excited squeals of laughter from a few of the people sitting in the chairs, none of whom looked like Polly. And then he spotted her, tucked away in the far back corner of the room, hidden from the light. As he neared her position he noticed a thick leather belt around her waist and others around her forearms, binding her to the chair. He spotted a bowl on a fixed shelf beneath her chair and realised with horror that she was strapped to a night commode. Her nightgown was hitched up at the back and around her skinny thighs, presumably so she could urinate straight into the pot below without having to be seen to.

Midnight was disgusted. Unexpected and unchecked fury rose from the depths of his soul and the few shadows in the room leaped to attention. The squeals of laughter quickly turned to ones of terror as Midnight tore at the straps restraining Polly. The sunlight in the room shrank from the dark, swirling masses that writhed over walls and floor towards him. His usually steady hands shook as he bent and scooped up the limp girl in his arms and carried her from the degradation.

Annie, Gredge and another male attendant came running towards the commotion, just as Midnight barrelled through the door cradling Polly. Annie shrieked.

"What the devil do you think you're doing? Put her down at once!"

Midnight shot her such a dark and furious look she physically cowered.

"Get whatever papers we need," he instructed her. "She's coming home with me. The other two as well."

"I say!" The other man interrupted.

"Who are you?" spat Midnight.

"I, sir, am the manager of this establishment and you cannot just remove patients under our care *willy-nilly!*"

"Care? Is *this* what you call care?" Midnight lifted Polly towards the flustered man. Gredge put a calming hand on his arm and whispered in his ear.

"Calm down man, look around you."

Midnight stole a glance at the walls and noticed more of the swirling shadows creeping towards them. He cursed under his breath. He needed to get his emotions under control. Taking in a deep, cleansing breath and pushing the shadows away, he lowered his gaze briefly before he next spoke.

"Mr...?"

"Hawksmith," the man offered hastily.

"Mr. Hawksmith. I am a very wealthy gentleman, one whom it would benefit you to... indulge. I am offering to take responsibility for three of your patients with immediate effect."

"But that is *not* procedure!" Hawksmith spluttered.

"This time it is. Make it so, with immediate effect, and I shall sign a cheque for one hundred pounds, payable to this establishment for the refurbishment of facilities and employment of sufficient staff so that *this*," he nodded towards Polly, "situation doesn't happen again."

Hawksmith's mouth hung open for the longest of moments before he clamped it shut and instructed Annie to ready the relevant paperwork.

"I'll be taking Miss Polly now, please get her belongings," Midnight told Annie who merely bobbed her head and scurried away, red-faced. To Hawksmith he said, "Mr. Bromley and Miss Sally will be sent for as soon as I can make rooms ready for them and hire a nurse. Have them escorted to this address. Arthur?"

Gredge wrote an address on his notepad, tore out the sheet and handed it to the dumbstruck manager.

Annie returned forthwith with a bundle of papers and a scratchy woollen blanket.

"She hasn't any belongings but I wrapped a clean night-shirt in here." She handed Gredge the blanket. Midnight placed Polly gently on a small armchair in the foyer and went with Hawksmith to sign the release documents, leaving Gredge and Annie to watch over her.

"We weren't trying to be cruel," Annie said, slightly abashed. "She's not like the rest, and they all have problems you know... but they can all sort of look after themselves. She doesn't really respond to us, she doesn't walk or talk. She just sits there, staring. We don't have enough staff to take care of her needs."

Arthur looked over at the frail little girl.

"*She,* is called Polly. I don't know how you've been caring for her, but I know Mr. Gunn. He is of outstanding moral fibre and one of the most generous souls I've ever had the pleasure of meeting. Rest assured, Polly will be very well cared for *now.*"

Annie fell quiet. Soon after, Hawksmith and Midnight returned. Scooping the girl back into his arms Gunn and Gredge left All Souls Pauper Asylum, without a backward glance.

9

CHANGES

"She's all settled now, sir." Clementine Phillips told Midnight as she exited a bedroom in the main wing of the Gunn mansion. Midnight stood outside the door waiting anxiously.

"Can I see her?"

"If you like, but she's sleeping. Maybe it's better to let the poor mite rest a while?"

"Yes, you're right of course Mrs. Phillips. I just wanted to check on her, that's all."

Mrs. Phillips laid a reassuring hand on her master's arm.

"She's as well as can be expected, after what you described of her troubles, sir. Sit with her if you must but let the little lamb rest. I will cook up some chicken broth ready for when she wakes. We must build up her strength. Doesn't look like she's had a decent meal in forever."

Midnight smiled. "You're a good-hearted woman Mrs. Phillips. Thank you. I will sit a while." He gently turned the door knob and pushed open the door quietly.

Polly lay in the grand four poster bed with a pristine white sheet drawn right up to her chin and a thick quilted bedspread

spread over the top and tucked in neatly along the edges. All he could see was a tiny pale face surrounded by a mass of dark hair. Her small frame looked lost in the huge bed, but she was safe and would be cared for as she deserved from now on. Midnight would see to it. Something stirred in him as he settled himself down in the chair beside her bed – an emotion he had not yet experienced but one he recognised from his contact with other people. He felt... *paternal* towards her. The realisation hit him with all the force of a blow to the gut, but he didn't reel from it. Instead he found that his heart had opened and he wanted nothing more than to embrace it. In contrast, his head warned him to steer clear of such reckless thoughts – the child would probably die, and sooner rather than later. *Unless I can save her,* he thought, *and the others too.* His thoughts turned to Bill Bromley and Sally. Giles and Mrs. Phillips had instructions to make up two more rooms in preparation for their arrival. Giles had put out an advert for a private nurse's position with board and pay but until the position was filled, they and Midnight would take responsibility for their care.

Some hours later, a gentle knock jolted him awake. He must have nodded off in the armchair during his vigil.

"Enter." Midnight said quietly, and Mrs. Phillips came in carrying a tray which she placed on the bedside table.

"Ah, she's waking up. 'Ello poppet, did you have a nice rest?" Mrs. Phillips smiled down at the girl and stroked her hair away from her face. The girl barely blinked, staring blankly at the ceiling. Midnight sat forward in his chair and looked at Polly. Her skin was ashen and her lips carried a slight blue tinge that put Midnight in mind of a fresh corpse. He frowned, not liking that he couldn't ascertain what was wrong with her.

"Your Lordship? Would you mind 'elping me prop her up

so I can spoon her some broth? Happen some decent food in her belly may warm her up."

Midnight jumped up and slid his arm around Polly's shoulders, lifting her. Mrs. Phillips positioned the pillows and Midnight sat Polly up against them. His hand brushed her forehead tenderly, which triggered a knowing smile from Clementine.

"Open up my little lamb," she raised a spoon to Polly's lips and the girl obediently slurped some broth. "I noticed when I tended to her earlier, if you ask her to do something she does it, though nothing of her own accord. It's very strange, sir."

"Indeed it is. I need some time with the girl when you feel she is ready please, Mrs. Phillips? I must figure this out if I'm to help her or the others."

"Of course. I'll need to tend to her personal needs once she's done with her dinner and then she'll be ready."

Midnight coughed. "Is everything prepared for our other guests?"

"Everything is ready. We'll manage between us, until the nurse arrives. Don't you worry now."

"Thank you Mrs. Phillips. I'll be in the library until then." He rose and started towards the door but paused and turned back towards his housekeeper, "I don't know how I'd cope without you and Giles. You really are a blessing." His words caused a bright blush to form on her cheeks, she smiled coyly and gave a deep, satisfied sigh. As Midnight closed the room door on his way out, he could've sworn he heard a quiet chuckle and a teasing "Scallywag" from Clementine.

THE GUNN LIBRARY was exactly as one would expect it to be in a grand house; full of old leather and cloth-bound volumes from floor to ceiling. Oak shelving covered every inch of wall space and in the centre of the room stood a great stone hearth and fireplace with a desk and two leather armchairs in the middle of an ornate woven rug. One door led through to a parlour that looked out onto the back garden and one led to the drawing room at the front of the house. A tall window let in the daylight at one end, and the other end opened on to a small ante-chamber which Midnight used as his study. It was to that room that he now headed. There, he turned to face another, smaller bookshelf and found the thick, red-faded volume halfway down the shelf. He pushed it firmly until it clicked and the sound of gears grinding rang loudly in the room. The bookshelf swung slowly inwards revealing a narrow stone staircase, that descended into the dark.

Midnight took the first few steps then reached above his head to pull the cord that dangled from the ceiling. Another click and the gears started up again, closing the door behind him. In the few seconds before the gaslight flickered into exis-tence, the shadows leaped for him excitedly but he blocked their advance and continued his descent.

At the foot of the staircase he pushed through another door and entered a wide underground basement. Upon the cold stone walls hung great, woven tapestries and a wide variety of mirrors. These mirrors were not for reasons of vanity, they were purely practical – there were no windows underground, so Midnight had adorned his secret room with mirrors to reflect as much light from the gas lamps and candles as possible. He did not like working with the shadows in his own house. Down here, he favoured the light.

Rummaging around in a desk drawer, he found what he was searching for. A gleaming amulet in the shape of a shining sun with a single white selenite stone, encased in iridium at its centre. He'd had no cause to use it for a long time, being quite adept in his powers now. This, he was sure, was what he needed to help him break through the block in Polly's mind.

A small brass ceiling bell rang inside the room. Midnight looked up at it. That must be Giles ringing to let him know Mrs. Phillips was finished with Polly. Placing the amulet around his neck he made his way back upstairs to the girl's room.

"All done," said Mrs. Phillips merrily. "She ate the lot!" She chuckled and waddled off down the corridor with the tray.

Midnight stepped into Polly's room eagerly, determined that he would shift the blockage so he could begin healing her. Pulling the chair closer to her bed, he perched on the edge of the seat. He drew in the light from the open window and calm settled over him. Opening his shirt a little, he tucked the sun-shaped pendant underneath it and gasped sharply as it adhered to his body, fusing with his skin right over his birthmark – the mark his old housekeeper, Mrs. Henshaw, had once thought of as the devil's own. What had started out as an inky and oddly shaped blot on his chest had changed and mutated as he'd grown. It now looked just like the shape of the sun merging with a comet. His father had given the pendant to him on his twelfth birthday; it helped him to enhance and concentrate on his burgeoning powers. It had been tucked away in that drawer for some time and Midnight knew he would need to charge the crystal with light before it would be useful. He drew in more of the sunlight that streaked across the bedroom and channelled it through the stone. It burned, but not unpleasantly – more like a concentrated warmth that radiated outwards in heat waves from its core.

The stone was ready and so was he. He drew in a deep breath and laid his palm on Polly's brow. He probed tentatively at first, allowing just a thin sliver of energy to flow into her, and felt for the blockage. It jerked and vibrated at his touch.

Yes! I see you. He let another thread of light join the first, controlling the way they twisted and combined to make a stronger one. Pushing again he felt the blockage shift and shrink. Encouraged he added a third thread and shoved a little harder. Polly twitched and her eyes shot towards him, piercing him with a wide-eyed stare. Then she screamed a long, loud and unfaltering wail, not unlike that of a banshee, that caused Midnight to startle and topple backwards over his chair. As soon as his eye contact with Polly broke, her screaming stopped. The noise and the clatter from the toppling chair had both Giles and Mrs. Phillips barrelling into the room just minutes later.

"My goodness, sir!" Giles exclaimed and hurried forward to help Midnight up off the floor.

"Is she alright? What happened?" screeched Mrs. Phillips, running to Polly's side and frantically patting her face and upper body as if looking for injury.

"She was defending herself, I was right! She's blocked her mind, put up a protective barrier against something – my guess is against whatever attacked her. I pushed at it and she looked straight at me. She *saw* me, I know she did!"

"Well why was she screaming like that?" Clementine asked.

"A warning I think. It started as soon as she made eye contact. Mrs. Phillips, Giles, we *have* to knock down that wall she has built inside her mind. She's in there somewhere and I think I can get her back!"

"That might well be, sir. But not today."

"But..."

"No! Begging your pardon, but no. The little lamb has suffered enough. I'll not have that screaming in this house again. She needs rest." Midnight had never heard Clementine Phillips sound so determinedly stern, she stood facing Giles and himself, her hands placed firmly on her hips, a thin-lipped scowl directed straight at him.

Having no choice but to retreat, Giles and Midnight left Polly to the tender attentions of the housekeeper. The butler made his way to the kitchen to finish his dinner, leaving Midnight alone on the upstairs landing. The scream had indeed startled him, and he wasn't entirely sure why she would react to him in such a defensive manner, only that she must be extremely frightened and confused. But she had *seen* him, the glazed look she normally carried had gone, albeit momentarily, and that was a breakthrough. *Next time it will work!* He vowed, *I will bring you back to the land of the living if it kills me.*

10

THE RAINBOW CLUB

They'd walked the length and breadth of the Limehouse backstreets, Gredge waiting outside each known opium den for Midnight to emerge with any leads, but so far none could be found.

"Either that," said Arthur, pointing to the little carved box in Midnight's hand, "means nothing to anyone or someone is lying."

"I'm rather inclined to feel it's the latter," Midnight replied. He'd just come from Fu Lee's; the last den on their list.

"What did Fu have to say about it?"

"Nice box but he knows nothing about any dragon-related club."

Gredge chuffed out a sigh.

"Same as the rest then!"

"What now?"

Gredge paused for a moment, thinking about his next move.

"Maybe we're asking the wrong people. Maybe we should be asking the patrons rather than the owners?"

"A stakeout!" Midnight declared gleefully.

"It's not as much fun as you think."

"Well that's because you've never been on one with me Inspector." Midnight's eyes twinkled.

"No funny business!"

"I'm quite sure I have no idea what you mean."

"Don't come the innocent with me, Gunn. I've seen you pull a few fast ones lately. I kept my mouth shut because, well, I know you did it for good reasons. But you can't go..." Arthur couldn't grasp the word he was looking for so he just shrugged instead and said, "You know... *messing about* with things."

"If by fast ones you mean the auction and the asylum, guilty as charged. However, I see those as necessary actions to facilitate the greater good."

"Cheating is what I call it, although I'm not adverse to seeing those big-wigs cop it from time to time. What you did for Polly and the others wasn't legal really. I mean, it is now you have the papers but you know... *how* you got them," he coughed and continued with caution; he knew how touchy Midnight got when they discussed his abilities. "Not exactly by negotiation or legal procedure, was it?"

"Are you asking or interrogating?"

"Asking."

Midnight nailed him with a piercing look.

"Shall we proceed with our *stakeout?*" He whispered the last word making it seem conspiratorial. "Minus any *funny business* obviously."

Arthur just shook his head. He knew he was getting no answers tonight.

"I mean it. I can bring you in to help decipher evidence and the like, but I can't have you intimidating information out of people, it wouldn't stand up. I have to keep things above board."

"Really?" Midnight's eyebrow arched reproachfully.

"As much as I'm able, yes!"

Midnight cocked his head in mock contemplation

"Oh bugger off man! You know what I mean."

"Oh yes, Arthur. I'm quite sure I do."

Arthur stomped off in a huff with a brooding Midnight following along behind. Together they made their way back through the cobbled streets of Limehouse to one of the most notorious opium hangouts, 'Wong's Emporium'. It doubled as a legitimate Chinese tea shop; selling traditional, imported teas and spices as well as teapots and cups, oriental statues, fans and paintings. Below, in the basement, was the opium den. Outside, just on the opposite corner in a darkening alley, Gredge and Gunn waited.

As late afternoon turned to early evening, the light dimmed, the shadows lengthened and Wong's Emporium now displayed a 'CLOSED' sign in its window. But that hadn't stopped one or two patrons from entering the shop via the basement door, which was situated below street level at the bottom of a small flight of stone steps. They'd watched a few Chinese fellows enter and a pair of Lascars – Indian sailors that crewed European ships – but Arthur felt that they wouldn't get the right answers from them. They needed...

"Him!" Gredge pointed towards a skinny-looking man in a worn day suit and bowler hat. The man looked nervous; he practically scurried down the street with his coat collar up and hat tipped down and every so often he'd glance around quickly as if to check he wasn't being followed. He had something tucked into his coat which he cradled with his arm.

"Shifty looking bleeder if ever I saw one."

"Shall we?" Midnight said and glided out of the alley towards the unsuspecting fellow.

"Good evening to you." Midnight greeted the man and stood directly in front of him, blocking his path. At first the man jumped at the sudden appearance and eyed him warily, but then seemed to soften as his took in Midnight's quality attire. This was clearly a gentleman and not some robber or blackguard. He cleared his throat.

"Good evening to you too, sir" he said, and made to step around. Midnight held out a hand appealingly.

"Might I trouble you a moment? You look like a helpful chap."

The man looked left and right but made no further attempt to move.

"What is it?"

"I'm looking for a particular establishment. One where a person might find some... relief." The man frowned but Midnight continued, "I'm sure you know what I'm referring to." He pointed towards the tea shop behind him, "I've seen one or two good gentlemen like yourself frequenting this establishment here and I wonder if it might be just the sort of place I'm looking for. That is where you were heading, am I correct?"

"I err, work for Mr. Wong yes," he replied and tightened his arm around whatever was stuffed under his coat. Midnight regarded him with steely aplomb. The look caused the man to take a step backwards and Gunn heard a loud cough from the alley where Gredge stood.

"Then you know *exactly* what I'm in need of?"

"Might I ask where you heard of Mr. Wong's, sir?"

"Ah, well, a good friend of mine gave me this," Midnight pulled out the wooden opium box that belonged to Emeline Rowbotham. "I was told to look for the dragon you see and, well, Mr. Wong has a dragon on his shop sign."

"Most Chinese shops have dragons on their signs." The man was starting to get suspicious, he shifted nervously on his feet. "This ain't the place you're looking for. Wong just sells teas and the like, is all. Sorry, I can't help you." And the man made to go around Midnight but was blocked by the sudden appearance of Inspector Gredge.

"Perhaps you can help me then, down at the station?"

"Oh buggering 'ell! I should've known you were a copper." He gave Midnight a reproachful glare.

"Oh I'm not, I'm just a citizen in need of directions. And you," he stepped closer to the man, "are going to help us."

"I already told you, I don't know what you mean!"

"What's in your coat?" Gredge asked and the man put his free hand over the bulge protectively.

"Nothin! It's personal."

"Well then if it's nothing you won't mind showing it to me eh?"

Reluctantly the man edged open his coat to reveal a velvet drawstring bag. It jangled as he moved.

"It's just some money I need to give to my employer is all. Takings... from the tea shop." He added quickly.

"From this tea shop?"

"Yeah."

"Hmm, I see and why would you be taking the takings back to the shop they supposedly came from?"

The man thought on his feet and answered,

"Bank's closed, innit? It was a last-minute bank run but I got delayed so I'm bringing them back." He nodded, clearly pleased with his fast thinking.

"The shop has been closed for over an hour," Gredge pointed out, "How were you planning on bringing them back?"

"Um," Midnight could fair hear the cogs grinding in the man's brain as he tried and failed to think of an answer that would suit.

"Where's the money from? You can either tell me here or back at the station, choice is yours." Said Gredge.

"Oh come on guv! I only do this to make extra for my family. I work down the docks as a clerk but it's poor wages and I got five kids to feed!"

"Better not let those five kids see their father in jail then, eh?"

"I ain't done nothin' wrong! It's just money runs is all. If Wong finds out I spoke to the rozzers I'll lose this job."

"Tell me where the money is from and I'll leave you be."

The man looked rapidly from Gredge to Gunn and back again, chewing his bottom lip.

"Fine! Wong's got another place, nothing like this one, up in Soho – 'The Rainbow Room'."

"Rainbow? That's an assembly hall!" Gredge declared. "Wong owns assembly rooms?"

"Yeah, that's the one. There's rooms upstairs for posh folk, like him. Wong doesn't own the whole thing, just the room upstairs." He nodded towards Midnight. "It's run by Chinese Mary but you'll need the password to get in."

"And that is?" Midnight asked.

"What's it worth?"

"Do you like prison food?" Gredge said, his tone full of impatience. The man mulled over his options. He realised they would not let him alone until he gave them what they wanted. The clock was ticking and Wong would be expecting his package; he wouldn't be pleased if he was late.

"That box of yours, show them that and give them the word 'Jiang', that'll get you in."

"Of course!" Midnight said, "Jiang is a double-headed dragon in Chinese mythology, it means *rainbow*, like the rainbow serpent."

"I dunno guv, I just know that's the password."

They let the man scurry off down the stone steps to Wong's basement and made their way to the nearest omnibus route that would take them to Soho.

Much to their disappointment the bus was a knifeboard and all the interior seats were taken. Midnight and Gredge hauled themselves up the iron rungs at the back of the carriage and onto the long bench on the roof. The three horses plodded along at a steady pace until they pulled up not far from where The Rainbow Room dominated the skyline on the south corner of Sutton Street and Soho Square. It was a grand building with arched windows and stone steps that led to black front door with a brass knocker. It looked more like a private house than an assembly room but for the small brass plaque on the door with the words 'Rainbow Rooms' engraved on it.

Gredge knocked and moments later the door opened and they were admitted to a small front parlour that acted as a kind of reception-come- sorting area. A smartly dressed clerk greeted them

"Good evening sirs, are you on the list?"

Gredge and Gunn looked at each other enquiringly.

"List?" Said Midnight

"Yes sir, the guest list."

"I was under the impression these were public assembly rooms, is this a private event?"

"The rooms are open to the public sir, yes, but one must apply for a season ticket to gain entry you see. I'm afraid if you don't have a ticket, well..." he shrugged apologetically. Midnight fished out the carved box and flashed it at the clerk,

"Will this do for a ticket?"

"I'm afraid I don't know what that is sir." he replied, his face the perfect picture of ignorance. "You can apply for membership if you would like to do so?" The clerk fished out a form and offered it to Midnight who shook his head politely and moved away to speak to his colleague quietly.

"Now what?"

"I don't know," Gredge shrugged, "It's not like I've ever been to one of these shindigs before."

"Neither have I!"

"I suppose I'll have to tell the clerk I'm on official police business then. Though I'd sooner not have to leave you behind, I feel like a fish out of water amongst all these aristocrats. What about the box?"

"No, he wasn't lying," Midnight said, nodding towards the busy clerk who kept intermittently looking at them over his half-moon glasses, "he really has no idea what it is. Not to put a damper on things Arthur, but I'd rather not have to register for a damned season ticket. This scene isn't my sort of thing."

"Ah! So, London's biggest mystery has revealed himself at last eh?" A booming voice bellowed all too close to Midnight's ear. He turned towards it and was greeted by a hearty clap on the shoulder from a bloated, toad-faced gentleman with greying hair wearing an evening suit that was clearly too small for his over-stuffed frame. Midnight was irked by the sudden intrusion but plastered a polite smile on his face nonetheless. "Aubrey Rudemeister," the toad said and held out his hand. Midnight shook it briefly while Rudemeister continued, "Yes, we were all extremely surprised by your fortuitous auction win! Quite the talk of London you are, sir. Mr. Gunn, isn't it?"

The question took Midnight by surprise, he hadn't met this man before, yet he seemed to know who he was.

"Yes, yes, it is. Midnight Gunn. I'm afraid I'm at a disadvantage Mr. Rudemeister, for you seem to know me but I believe we are not yet acquainted. Am I mistaken?"

"No, no. You are correct in your assumption dear boy. We are not yet acquainted, but I did know your father somewhat.

Very sad, his passing, very sad indeed. Tragic. No, you see you caused quite the stir in the auction house, not many can say they took on the East India Company and won! People wanted to know who you were but of course... all secret and the like, eh?" Aubrey Rudemeister chortled and winked. "I knew. Took me a while but I got it in the end. Recognised the chap who sat with you, I did!"

Midnight looked at Arthur who just shrugged. Aubrey laughed brash and loud.

"Good heavens no! Not this one, don't know who he is. Your butler! Gerald or something, isn't it?"

"Giles" Midnight corrected.

"That's the fellow! Giles, very efficient, yes. Always accompanied your father... towards the end. Highly unusual having a *butler* accompany his master during a business transaction, of course. Quite eccentric really." He shook his head in a disapproving manner which made Midnight's annoyance turn almost menacing in defence of his father and Giles, but he managed to hold it in after a swift kick on the shin from Gredge. The shadows on the parlour walls immediately receded. Midnight didn't trust himself to speak, so after a moment of awkward silence that Rudemeister seemed blatantly unaware of, it was Arthur that broke it,

"Are you going in then? To the ball?"

He was rewarded with a look of clumsily guarded disdain before Rudemeister remembered his manners and replied,

"Indeed yes, er...Mister?"

"Detective Inspector Gredge."

"Oh! Oh my, well that would explain it then. Ha! Good lord I thought he was your driver or something." Rudemeister directed his comment at Midnight who did not reply but barely managed not to glare at his ill-mannered company. "Yes, I am attending the ball tonight, always do, every

Wednesday throughout the season. Alas my good wife couldn't make it tonight she is feeling unwell but my daughter is here somewhere," he paused to look, "I say, I heard the clerk fellow say that you were not on the guest list, am I right?"

"Unfortunately yes. I am not usually one for social gatherings."

"Indeed, indeed. In light of my dear wife's absence, I could have you accompany me as *my* guest? Of course, I couldn't really take your companion. Not proper you know." He indicated apologetically at Gredge's clear lack of suitable evening attire.

"No need to worry sir, I'm conducting an investigation. I won't need an invitation." Gredge's reply was polite but curt. The toad nodded but continued to look doubtful. Most of the upper classes regarded the police as not much better than a common clerk. The lower classes mostly hated them. As high ranking as a Detective Inspector was, he might still have a hard time gaining entry to the exclusive event.

"You go with Mr. Rudemeister and I'll see you inside." Gredge instructed Midnight, who nodded.

"If you're sure Arthur?"

"Of course, go ahead. I'll go have a little word with the clerk. It's probably best if we're not seen together anyway."

Rudemeister clapped Midnight on the back and guided him enthusiastically into the corridor that led to the large assembly rooms. Gredge smirked, knowing full well that his friend would be cringing at the brashness of his new companion. If there was one thing Midnight hated, it was to be the centre of attention.

11

CHINESE MARY

Midnight had endured the introductions to various members of London's wealthiest families as best he could. But he could stomach the polite conversation and simpering duplicity no longer. Gredge had not appeared and so he made his excuses to Rudemeister and went in search of the Inspector. He made his way around the room, deftly avoiding anyone who looked vaguely interested in starting a conversation with him, and spotted Gredge standing in a corner near a very big potted cheese plant, looking vexed.

"There you are! What on earth are you wearing?"

"I should've thought that obvious." Gredge replied in a clipped tone. Midnight covered his mouth to hide a grin. "It's not funny! I feel ridiculous." Gredge fidgeted, pulling angrily at the sleeves on an overly large evening jacket which in turn caused the top hat he now sported instead of his usual bowler to topple sideways.

"It's rather a poor attempt at a disguise Arthur, I must say."

"Bloody clubs and their bloody dress codes! I had to borrow this garb from the lost property room. It seems the clerk was concerned that having a plain-clothes policeman in plain sight would upset the guests! Wouldn't want that now, would we?" he added, the sarcasm dripping from his tongue.

"Are you going to stop hiding behind this poor plant? I think the sight of you is causing it to wilt."

"Funny." Gredge gave Midnight a scathing look and edged out from the corner. "Are you ready to find this bloody secret club then or what?"

"Of course. The stairs leading to the upper floors are to the right. From what I can gather, this used to be a residential building but the interior has been converted and altered quite a bit. There's another smaller room through that archway that is only accessed via a bridge."

"A bridge in a house?"

"I know, it's quite vulgar. Much like many of the guests it seems."

"Quite the social snob, aren't you?" Gredge scoffed.

"I abhor these types of gatherings Arthur. Nothing but an excuse to posture and flaunt one's wealth and social standing."

"I would've thought you would need to mingle occasionally to maintain your father's business connections?"

"I prefer to conduct my business matters on a one-to-one basis and usually through my lawyer. I admit, I do rely on Father's good name probably more than I should and thus far it has worked. I blame *you* entirely for exposing me in this highly audacious manner. I've already had to suffer several invitations to dinners which I have no intention of attending."

"Why is it my fault? You're as invested as I in this investigation! You need to venture out of the woodwork now and again. People will think you're a ghost."

"I'd prefer it if they did. Now, let's get on with this before some unfortunate lady solicits a dance!"

They left the noise and throng of the ground floor gath-

ering and made their way as inconspicuously up the staircase as they could. One or two gentlemen passed them on
their way down with a knowing nod. The stairs took them
past the first floor, where the men's restroom and ladies
powder rooms were, to the second where they alighted onto
a darkened landing. Most of the windows had heavy velvet
curtains drawn across shutting out the view of the street
below. The music and chatter from beneath them fell
behind as they made their way along the corridor. There
were no hall tables or occasional chairs, no furnishings or
wall decorations of any kind. It was designed to make any
wandering guests think it a redundant space and not worth
further investigation. The walls were drab with peeling
paint, faded wallpaper and dusty runners on the floor. There
were no exposed doors to speak of, but more heavy velvet
curtains hung over the suggestion of what looked to be a
wide frame set at the far end of the passage. Midnight
grasped the cloth and tugged it aside exposing a rather
plain-looking door.

"Shall we?" Midnight indicated to Arthur to open the door

"Isn't there a secret knock or something? There usually is."
Arthur replied in droll tones.

"Probably, but we have the key!" said Midnight, patting the
pocket of his evening coat where the small wooden box lay.
Arthur's mouth skewed at the side as he rapped loudly twice
on the door. Nothing happened. He knocked again and they
heard shuffling on the other side, but still nobody opened it.
Arthur ran his hand over the top half of the door and found a
small spy hole. The darkness of the corridor made it almost
impossible to see but it was there.

"Pass me the box?" Arthur held out his hand for it and
then waved it in front of the peep hole. They heard more shuffling and a bolt slide open before the door opened just enough

for a heavy-set Chinese man to poke his face out and scowl at them.

"Who are you?" he demanded.

"We're patrons of the club," Arthur replied and wiggled the box at the man whose scowl merely deepened.

"Wait," he said. Then slammed the door and bolted it.

"Bloody brilliant. We'll be here all night at this rate."

"Patience Arthur. The man said wait, so we wait."

"Patience isn't one of my virtues I'm afraid."

"I noticed."

They waited outside the door for a further ten minutes before the bolt rattled again and the door swung open to allow them entry. The doorman let them draw level with him then flung out a hand and said,

"You come see Mrs. Mary now." He shuffled off before they even had chance to reply, leaving them no choice but to follow. The doorman led them into a small room laid out like a parlour and lavishly decorated in rich scarlet fabrics and gilded fretwork panels. Chinese lanterns hung from the ceiling casting a dim warm glow around the room. Both Arthur and Midnight were surprised to find that Chinese Mary, the woman who reportedly ran the establishment, wasn't Chinese at all but was in fact unequivocally English. She greeted them like any other well-bred English lady would, with a delicate smile and a gloved hand, which Midnight took and gently kissed and Arthur shook reluctantly.

"Well, gentlemen. Now the niceties are over perhaps you'd be so kind as to tell me who you are and why you have Miss Rowbotham's members' box?" Her tone was pleasant but Midnight detected a trace of warning in it that indicated she was not as delicate as she might appear. His quick senses recognized that they were not the only people in the room. He felt hidden eyes watching them from behind the elaborate panelling. There was no point in lying to her, she already knew they weren't patrons. Honesty would have to get them access now.

"So much for incognito." Arthur said under his breath and promptly removed his oversized topper from his head with a certain degree of relief. Midnight noted that his colleague's demeanour improved once he was back in his comfortable role as Detective Inspector. "My name is Inspector Gredge of Scotland Yard, this is... Detective Gunn. We're here to investigate the murder of Miss Rowbotham." If he was hoping for the bluntness of his declaration to shock their host, he was mistaken. The news didn't seem to be new to her.

"You already knew." Midnight stated. Mary nodded.

"Of course I did. I know everything about my clients, *Detective* Gunn." The emphasis on his fake title wasn't lost on Midnight. Mrs. Mary was quite a wily woman underneath her perfectly coiffed blonde curls and flawless make up. He made a mental note not to underestimate her.

"Perhaps you could tell us how she ended up strangled to death in a Southwark alley then?" Arthur quipped.

"Touché Inspector Gredge. When I said everything, I meant everything worth knowing. How the poor girl ended up dead is not my concern. Her debts have been paid and she was removed from my client list. I had already been informed her passkey," she glanced at the wooden box in Arthur's hand, "was in the possession of the police." Gredge found her smug smirk disconcerting.

"Who and how?" he demanded.

"Now Inspector, did your mother never instruct you in the proper use of manners? Tsk tsk." She reached for a lace fan atop an ornate ebony table and casually flipped it open, wafting it slowly. The gentle brush of air from the fan made her curls dance and sway and Midnight found himself momentarily distracted by it. He caught himself looking and quickly redirected his gaze at Arthur who was gradually losing patience with her game.

"Madam, please. It's been a long day and Inspector Gredge and I are merely chasing justice for poor Miss Rowbotham. This passkey is an important piece of evidence that led us to you. We're not interested in how you run this place or what goes on here but I'm sure the Superintendent might be. So, unless you want a bunch of policemen at your door, I'd suggest you give us your full co-operation. We understand you aim to keep your client records confidential, but we must know who paid her debts and how you knew we had the box."

"Oh you *must*? Well then," she challenged.

"I absolutely insist." Whether it was something in his tone or the sudden shadow that passed over his face, he didn't know but her confident defiance slipped to be replaced by unexpected wariness and willingness to comply with his demands. She shifted awkwardly in her seat, looking rapidly between Gredge and himself. He heard rustling and a discreet cough from behind the fretwork panels, but Mary held up her hand, halting the advance of the protector hidden there.

"Give me a few moments to retrieve the information, gentlemen?" she waited for them to acquiesce to her request before continuing. "Perhaps the detectives might enjoy some refreshments in the members lounge while they wait? Kim, would you kindly show these gentlemen to a booth?" A large man emerged from the fretwork, dressed in black silks and tunic with a shaven head and long plaited beard, he stood level with Midnight but infinitely bigger in build. He made for quite an imposing figure. Now it was Gredge's turn to cough.

"I suppose I could use a drink," he said.

"I'll send Kim when I have the information you require." Mary told them as they were ushered through a door into a large elaborately decorated lounge area. Bawdy music hall tunes danced through the air, cloudy with the sweet-smelling smoke of the opium pipes. Men and women in various attire and state of undress were littered around the main area chatting and laughing.

"This way." Kim grunted and pointed forwards. Midnight and Arthur made their way across the room to the far side where several private booths lay in relative darkness. Each booth was encompassed by the same fretwork panelling that adorned Mary's parlour. Kim opened the door to the booth in the corner that faced away from the main lounge and Gredge and Gunn took a seat on a red chaise with gold braiding. Midnight took stock of the intricately embroidered tapestries that adorned the wall. All depicted scenes of a highly sexual nature; bare-breasted women with wine goblets in one hand and an opium pipe in the other. Another showed a male figure with his head buried between a woman's legs and a third tapestry showed two naked men draped over a bed enveloped in each other's arms.

Kim bowed and informed them he would send a tray with refreshments. Midnight noticed Arthur's gaze drift to the tapestries and a flush spread rapidly across his cheeks. He smiled inwardly as Arthur cleared his throat and averted his gaze to anywhere but the wall. Music and animated chatter filled the awkward silence until a scantily-clad woman appeared with two glasses and Absinthe apparatus. She expertly prepared the concoction for them, much to Arthur's horror, before leaving with a wink and a smile in Midnight's direction.

"Couldn't she have brought beer? I wouldn't touch this stuff if you paid me." Arthur said, pushing his glass away.

"When in Rome!" Midnight replied and raised his glass to

his friend in mock salute. "Mm, it's a little bitter on the after-taste but gives one quite a pleasant tingle."

"You can keep your tingle, I'll stick to the amber stuff down the pub. How long are we going to have to wait here? How bloody long does it take to find a bit of information?"

"Oh I daresay our lovely hostess already knew what we were seeking but she's not going to give it up without a price."

"What do you mean?"

Midnight tapped his glass.

"It's drugged."

"What?" Arthur shot forward in his seat and reached for the glass.

"No, Arthur. It's alright, I must finish it."

"Why the bleeding hell must you?"

"Because if at least one of us doesn't, I suspect you may not make it out of here alive." Midnight whispered in dramatic fashion and then giggled like a school boy, "You look like you just sucked a sour lemon, ha!"

"What the blazers is in that drink? You've come over all... all *funny*." Arthur was incredulous, he made another attempt to snatch away the glass.

"Do be a good chap and let me finish it? The sooner we get this charade over with the better for you."

Arthur scowled and lowered his voice,

"And why is it only me that's not going to make it out alive then?"

"Because Mary knows I'm not a detective, you're the one who poses the most danger to her business and I suspect she knows more than she's letting on about our secret debt payer. She means to get rid of us as quickly as possible. I believe her aim was to drug us and probably have Kim and Co dump our bodies in the Thames. This way, if I'm drugged and you're not she only has one option left."

"Which is?"

"To hold me captive until you drop this line of enquiry and give her time to move her business elsewhere." Midnight took another big slurp of the Absinthe cocktail.

"How can you tell all of that just from being here for twenty minutes?"

Midnight raised a finger to his temple.

"I sense things remember? Superpowers and what not." He slurred and his eyes rolled as he fought to stay conscious.

"Oh shite! Midnight? Stay awake man! What should I do?" He shook his friend.

"Play along, agree to whatever she demands. Don't worry about me, I have this all in hand." And then his head slumped forward and hit the table. A moment later, the booth door flung open and Gredge's skull connected with something hard. He turned just in time to see a grinning Kim, club raised for another blow if necessary, before he too passed out cold.

12

DECEPTION

His peripheral vision took longer to return, the vignette that hampered his sight was disconcerting at first, as was the heavy fog that clouded his ability to think clearly. He had to draw in the light from the candles surrounding the bed he was laid on to speed up the healing process. Then he remembered; he was at Chinese Mary's Rainbow Club, he'd been drugged, and by now – hopefully – Arthur was long gone and would be eagerly awaiting his return, however long that may take.

Rustling on his right side alerted him that he was not alone and the tell-tale shuffle of feet told him it was probably Kim. Careful not to appear too alert, he let out a soft groan. Kim appeared and stood bent over him, squinting. He reached out and took Midnight's face in one meaty hand and slapped him hard with the other. Midnight groaned again and Kim muttered something in Chinese, he heard a door open and shut and then the distinct perfume of a woman wafted through the air towards him.

"Thank you Kim, you may go." Mary instructed. Kim began to protest but was silenced by a wave of her hand.

"Leave us! He's in no fit state to be any threat. He'll be like this for hours." Kim left, and Mary strolled victoriously to the door and locked it. "Well now *Detective* Gunn," she said silkily, "you've gone and got yourself into a bit of a fix it seems. Whatever am I to do with you?" The mattress dipped as she sat down next to her captive, her hand strayed towards his neck and she ran a finger in a slashing movement across it.

"Where... am I?" Midnight muttered sluggishly. Mary placed her hand on his cheek and stroked it soothingly

"Shush now handsome, no need to fret. Mary will look after you. You're going to be very... very comfortable here." She moved her hand down towards his chest and toyed with his top shirt button. Popping it open and moving to the next one, her tongue left a wet trail on her bottom lip. She finished undoing his shirt and pushed it open to expose his torso. Midnight could sense her pulse quicken at the sight of him and still fighting for control over the drug, his body responded of its own accord. Mary noticed at once and her breath hitched. She took his reaction to mean that he welcomed her attentions and grew bolder. Rising, Mary hitched up her skirts and straddled him. Rocking her pelvis back and forth with mounting confidence she began to laugh,

"Why sir, you *are* pleased to see me."

"Arthur?"

"Arthur! Ha! Surely not? I am certain Mr. Midnight that your affections for your dear detective do not run *that* deep?"

"Where is he?" His voice rose a little too much, his agitation noticeable. Mary stiffened.

"He's gone. He's no longer your concern. You however, seem to be a little too perky for my liking. Kim! Kim!" She scrambled off Midnight and a moment later Kim blundered through the door.

"Yes lady?"

"Bring him another dose. He grows restless."

"Yes lady." Kim turned to leave,

"Make it a bigger dose this time. He's stronger than I thought."

As soon as the door closed she turned back to the bed where Midnight lay, struggling to get up. A second later Mary fished out a short, thick wooden club from a hidden pocket in her skirts and lashed out as hard as she could. It connected with his temple and once again he lay still.

"Feisty one, aren't you?" Mary said to a motionless Midnight, "I like my men with a little fire in their bellies." She ran the club slowly down from the bridge of his nose to the waistband of his trousers as Midnight lay unmoving, his breathing shallow. "What am I to do with you? Your little inspector friend had to go but you... you're just too pretty to let go just yet. Besides, a girl must have an insurance policy. I can't have people turning up uninvited and asking questions they have no business asking." Mary bent and kissed Midnight on the mouth. He tasted divine – bittersweet. She let her tongue travel over his bottom lip, the club dropped from her hand and landed with a dull thud on the rug. Her hands went to his hair and her fingers grabbed handfuls and tugged him closer. The taste of him did something to her, drew her in, it was intoxicating and confusing. She wanted to devour him right there, right now, the fact he was unconscious didn't even enter her head, so addictive was his flavour. Heat flooded her veins, everything grew dim and all she could focus on was kissing him. Mary didn't notice the shadows in the room creep ever closer, inch by inch they swirled towards the bed. A churning maelstrom of dark fury bore down on her, ready to pounce. The moment struck when she forced her hungry tongue past her captive's silent lips to explore his mouth further. Midnight's eyes flew open and the shadows slammed into his body. The instinct to resist such an assault caused him to bite down on the thing that invaded his mouth. The next thing he tasted was blood. Mary reeled from him, her hands flying to her mouth. Blood poured through her fingers and she stumbled to the floor in horror. Midnight sprang from the bed, his fierce stare fixed on her and spat. A pink chunk of flesh landed on the floor next to the frantic woman- it was her tongue.

The dark power of the shadows roiled inside of him and he fought for control. He usually had time to prepare himself for the invasion but this time they'd leaped upon him without an invitation. If the truth be known, he found it a little disconcerting yet also reassuring, as he now knew his plan had worked. Only once before, in his childhood, had the shadows taken him over uninvited and it had almost killed him. He'd been unconscious then too, knocked out after a riding accident, his powers had leapt to his defence and protected him from the raging bull in the farmer's field. The force of the shadows' rage had rendered him comatose for almost a month after. He was thankful that had not been the case this time and briefly wondered why.

His attention returned to the mewling, sobbing Mary who now scurried backwards on her bottom, attempting to get away from him. Blood spurted from her mouth and covered her gown, hands, chin and neck. She couldn't scream for Kim –her tongue was gone and she spluttered and choked on the blood that filled her mouth. She was trying to get to the bell pull by the door.

"Oh I don't think so madam!" Midnight shot out both his hands and channelled his power. Mary was hoisted off the floor by a spinning mass of charcoal-black smoke and flung against the wall where she remained, arms outstretched like the crucifixion of Christ, as her life's blood dripped down the wall and onto the floor. The door handle turned but Midnight was fast and focused now, the power burned inside him but he didn't care. He fired another stream of smoke at Kim as he entered; it looped around his wrist and dragged the struggling heap-of-a-man through the doorway. Kim's angry expression turned to one of horror when he saw the state of his mistress pinned to the wall. He tried to reach her but Midnight's hold on him was too great.

"You will give me the information I want *now!*" Midnight's tone was fixed and unyielding and Kim's eyes widened when a thin trail of the smoke that pinned Mary wound its way around her neck and tightened.

"I give you nothing! You leave her or friend die!"

"What do you mean?" Midnight faltered, a small flutter of concern in his chest.

Kim squinted at him and said in clipped English,

"You let her go or detective friend *dies!*"

"You're bluffing. You don't have him." His reply was bold but in the back of his mind he heard Mary's earlier words *'He's gone, he's no longer your concern.'* And he knew it was no ruse. The big oaf started to laugh. He knew Midnight had no choice but to let them both go. He didn't know that his foe barely held control over the power within and his mocking laughter had just tipped him over the edge.

An outraged roar sprang from Midnight, a wave of dark power rode the cacophony of sound. Other screams rent the air, but he was oblivious to them, intent only on ending his adversaries. Bones snapped and bodies crumbled to the ground. Behind his enraged glare, Midnight reeled and struggled for control. It was as if he were watching through somebody else's eyes. He was not a killer but at this moment his powers had deceived him – they were in command. His veins pulsed and his body quivered as he pushed back at the shadows; they were reluctant to give way now that they finally had free rein to do as they willed. Midnight looked at the inert bodies of Mary and Kim. They were barely breathing. If he didn't stop his onslaught now they would die. He pushed again but his powers hardly shifted. Trying not to panic, Midnight focused his mind's eye and tried to look past the darkness within. Then an idea came to him – *the light!* There were candles dotted around the room. He knew he must channel the light to fight the dark. He'd never held both sides of his powers inside before, he wasn't sure if he even could, but he knew he must try or death would once again be on his hands. The image of that fateful night in his childhood haunted him; his father clutching his chest, the darkness raging uncontrollably through him and his father pleading with his dying breath *'accept it my son, death is but a part of life, you must... accept it.'* That was one death he would never accept. His father died because of him and he'd vowed then never to let his powers overwhelm him to the point that they became more powerful than his own will. It was this notion that forced Midnight to suck in the light from the candles now. No matter how much danger he found himself in or however much people deserved to feel his wrath, he would not kill.

Like a worm burrowing through black soil, the light wriggled its way to his core and began to spread. The dark resisted – screamed in defiance – but it was losing. Midnight could feel the light's warmth coursing through him, spreading its soothing balm until the shadows finally relented and let go.

His victims lay quiescent, the atmosphere baited and soundless for the few moments it took Midnight to take stock of the situation. *What have I done?* Dashing towards an unconscious Kim, he bent and felt for a pulse. *Thank God!* Next, he went to Mary, who was in a far worse state. He channelled the light and sent her enough healing to stem the blood flow and quicken her heartbeat. She would live. He knew he needed to leave and now, before any more of Mary's henchmen appeared. He hadn't gotten the information he wanted but that was of little consequence now he knew that something had happened to Arthur. He must find his friend. What would happen when Mary and Kim awoke? They would surely kill the Inspector out of revenge! He couldn't take the risk and that left him only one option: he would have to addle their minds. It was not an option that appealed to his morals but it was infinitely better than killing them both and it was his only way of keeping Arthur safe – wherever he was.

He felt great trepidation knowing that the only way he could find out what had happened to Arthur was to call upon the shadows once more. He needed to see into their memories – just like he had with the unconscious Spring-heeled Jack victims. He steadied himself, taking deep regulating breaths. He could not afford to allow those shadows to command him again. He let go of the light and saw the shadows twitch in anticipation. Carefully and slowly he let them in. It was more painful than ever before – they burned and stabbed at his insides, desperately wanting the freedom they'd just tasted but he managed to rein them in. Once in control, Midnight laid a hand on Mary's forehead. Images flooded his mind, snippets of her day-to-day dealings, faces of prominent clients, her sexual exploits and then finally glimpses of Arthur. He saw his friend being rolled up in blankets and dragged down a corridor and Kim hoisting the bundle on his shoulders and throwing him down a dark set of stairs into what looked like a cellar. He focused hard on the blurry memory.

"Nobody find him lady, we get away before he found."

"Tell no one Kim, do you understand? I will send an anonymous letter to Scotland Yard once we are gone. A shame we can't kill him but I've no way of knowing how many of them knew he was coming and I'd rather not have a murder charge on my head. He'll

be awake in a day or two and by then we will be gone when they come for him."

"Yes lady, what about other man? You should put him here too, he dangerous, Kim knows."

"We need to take him with us as insurance, just in case something happens or someone else comes before we move the operation out. I might keep him... or kill him if he proves to be trouble."

"He works for police?"

"Oh Kim, he's no more a policeman than you or I! He's a gentleman, which means he has money. He may yet be of use if we could ransom him, who knows."

The cellar door slammed and was padlocked and the memory faded. Before he let go, Midnight sent a small ball of his power into the centre of Mary's mind and left it there to eat away at her memories. She would forget all about him and Arthur and possibly everything else, but it was a risk he was prepared to take. He would find Arthur himself, whatever it took. He wouldn't kill these two but he couldn't let them go either because they would go straight to Arthur and finish him. No, this was his only option. Perhaps Kim's memories would give him more clues. He turned to the large motionless hulk behind him and stopped. Something was wrong. Midnight lowered himself to his knees and tentatively reached for Kim. A horrible sinking cold dread filled his gut. He touched Kim's forehead and immediately recoiled. Kim was dead.

13

TWO FACES OF EVIL

The rain poured down, soaking him through, but he didn't notice. He had left his coat, shoes and hat behind, having neither time nor inclination to search for them. He ran through the streets, barefoot. His trousers were saturated and muddy, his open shirt clung to his skin. He ran past cabs carrying passengers, thankful that the weather meant there were few pedestrians. He did not want to be among people, he didn't deserve to be. He was a murderer. The night cloaked him, but he felt more conspicuous than ever. The glow of the streetlamps felt like glaring stage lights casting judgement on his dastardly deed. Home, he needed to get home. He would look for Arthur as soon as he could, but now he just needed to be inside his own four walls. Midnight continued running until the bricks and mortar became familiar – Piccadilly, then Old Bond Street, before turning towards Berkeley Square and home. Meriton House, the Gunn residence, stood proud and tall behind a red brick wall and arched iron gates. He came to a standstill on the pavement outside and looked upon it. The rain still poured and he let it drench him further, wishing to wash away his guilt. He needed to feel cleansed before entering. He couldn't be near the innocent souls that abided inside.

Stepping through the gates towards the front door he hoped that Giles and Mrs. Phillips were in bed, he couldn't face either of them this evening. The creak of the door resonated through the hallway and he cringed. He walked quietly towards the stairs and made it to the third step when a voice rang out behind him,

"Sir? Is that you?" Giles held aloft a small oil lamp and Midnight shied away, shielding his eyes from the glow. "Where the blazes have you been? We've been worried sick!" Midnight was taken aback by the tone in Giles' voice. He dropped his arm and peered at his butler.

"What on earth are you talking about? I often return home late. What's happened? Is it Polly?" He spun around and began leaping up the stairs two at a time before Giles called him back,

"Sir! You've been gone three days!"

"Three days? That's impossible! Why I only left the house this morning!" Midnight scurried back down to the hallway and grabbed Giles by the shoulder.

"Today is Friday sir, you left on Wednesday morning. Mrs. Phillips made me contact Detective Gredge, but he has not yet replied to my note. The poor woman has been beside herself."

The gravity of what Giles was telling him sank in. If he'd been gone three days that meant that Arthur had been unconscious in a cellar all that time! Nobody had looked for him, nobody knew where he was or if he was still alive!

"Dear God, Giles I must leave at once! Arthur is missing, he needs me!"

"Oh no young master! You are not going anywhere until you explain yourself, have something to eat, bathe, and are properly attired!" Came the high-pitched reply of a very irate

Mrs. Clementine Phillips. "And what's more, there's a young girl upstairs that needs you. Your detective friend can wait."

"Mrs. Phillips, you don't understand, Inspector Gredge is in trouble. He may not even be alive! I *must* find him." Midnight pleaded, feeling a little like a child being scolded by his mother.

"If that is the case your Lordship, might I suggest forming a search and rescue plan? One simply can't just rush out into the rain half-dressed and have a missing person materialize out of thin air. Do you even know where he is?" Giles asked.

"Sort of... no, not really. He's in a locked cellar somewhere but that's all I know."

"Then nothing can be gained by leaving now. I will draw you a bath..."

"No! No time for that." Midnight cut in.

"Very well, no bath... but I will have you in clean, dry clothes and for goodness sake let Mrs. Phillips feed you before she has an apoplectic fit. Then we shall sit down and see what is to be done for the Inspector."

"Yes, fine, but we must waste no time Giles, this is a matter of urgency!"

"Indeed, sir. Let's start by getting you out of those wet clothes, shall we?"

"I'll go warm up some soup," said Mrs. Phillips, "and mind you pop in and see the young mistress when you're dressed!"

"Thank you Mrs. Phillips, I will. Giles, I need to get a message to Scotland Yard. And Constable Rowe, he'll want to help I'm sure."

"I'll send out a runner as soon as you're dressed sir."

"No, do it right away please Giles, I can find my own clothes. This is more important."

"As you wish sir." Giles tilted his head in compliance and left Midnight to tend to himself.

Midnight stripped off his wet clothes and dressed hastily, eager to make rescue plans and to see young Polly. If he'd been gone three days it was possible she had made some improvement on her own but he doubted it. He'd wanted to try another healing as soon as possible but now Arthur needed to be found it would have to wait.

Mrs. Phillips brought him up some warmed soup and a hot bread roll and he wolfed it down appreciatively, not realizing till that moment how hungry he was.

"Superb as always, thank you dear Mrs. Phillips. How is Polly doing? Has she shown any improvement?"

"I suppose you're about to find out." She gave him a warm smile and took his bowl from him.

"Let's go and see, shall we?" Midnight held open his door for Clementine as she carried his supper tray to a small side table on the landing and set it down.

"I think you'll be pleasantly surprised sir, she's a proper poppet is Miss Polly."

"That sounds encouraging indeed! All down to your expert care no doubt."

"Well, I ain't usually one to blow my own trumpet but 'appen all that young 'un needed was some hot food, a safe bed and a bit o' love! By the looks of her she's had not much of that in her life." Mrs. Phillips shook her head. "Poor little mite."

"We must make sure there's plenty of those things and more in her future then."

"Indeed young master, indeed. You are a kind soul." Mrs. Phillips paused outside Polly's room and pressed her hands together, "Now, if you please sir, I think it best if I pop in first and tell her she has a visitor. No offence mind, but she doesn't exactly know you very well."

"I think it best dear Clementine."

"Mrs. Phillips if you please sir. I might be just a cook and housekeeper, but I know how to keep things proper." Her words were chastising but Midnight couldn't help but notice her cheeks flush and her mouth twitch.

"You're more than just a cook and housekeeper dear lady," he patted her arm affectionately. "How about we settle on Mrs. P?" He winked and before she could chastise him again, quickly followed with "I do believe Miss Polly is waiting." Mrs. Phillips gave a gentle knock before entering the bedroom and closed the door behind her. Midnight could hear her chatting to Polly and the sound of the child's voice pleased him. He hadn't ever thought she would make a recovery of her own accord. He wondered if the other victims had made such progress and made his mind up to check up on them once Arthur had been found.

The door opened and Mrs. Phillips beckoned him in. He stood just inside the doorway behind his housekeeper as she began to introduce him.

"Now then Miss, this is the Master; Mr. Gunn. It is in his house you reside now."

"Should she wish to of course." Midnight interjected, still somewhat obscured by the door and Mrs. Phillips' rather rotund frame.

"Yes, should you wish to remain in our care obviously. The master is a good man and provides a good home. I'm sure you'll find him kindly enough."

Midnight stepped into full view and flashed his best welcoming smile at Polly who seemed to smile back, albeit a little nervously. It took mere seconds for the mood in the room to change, for when Polly's eyes met his she began screaming frantically and backed away. She scrambled off her bed and dove under it, shouting over and over,

"Get away! Get away!"

"Oh my goodness! What on earth's gotten into you girl?" Mrs. Phillips dropped to her knees and peered under the bed. Midnight was horrified! Was he really that frightening? He couldn't fathom why the girl kept reacting to him so, he'd been nothing but kind to her.

"I think I'd better go. Should I fetch Giles?"

"I'll calm her down sir, just give me a moment. Come now Miss Polly, there's nothing to fear, it's just the master."

The girl continued to scream.

"I really don't think she wants me here. I will leave. I need to talk to Giles anyway. Perhaps I'll try a visit another day." And with that he darted from the room and closed the door. Polly still screamed and he could hear poor Mrs. P. desperately trying to calm her. The girl's reaction upset him greatly. Perhaps he really was a monster? Perhaps she could sense he was a killer and that's why she was frightened of him? The front door bell clanged making him jump. At this late hour, it could only be Constable Rowe. *Thank God!* He would put his time to better use and get started on the hunt for Arthur. He made for the stairs in haste.

"Giles? Is that the Constable?" He heard the front door creak as he descended.

"It is sir."

"Rowe? Welcome, do come in." Midnight gestured for him to enter. "Let's go to the front parlour. Giles, please have Mrs. Phillips bring some tea and join us if you would?"

"Of course sir."

Midnight noticed the swift frown cross Rowe's brow, he realized his request for Giles to accompany them would seem wholly out of place. One usually didn't include a butler in such matters. No matter, there was no time to explain their unique relationship now. Time was not on Arthur's side. They must make plans immediately.

"This way Constable. I'm anxious to talk with you. Apologies for the late hour but I assume you're aware of the urgency of my summons?"

"I am indeed Mr. Gunn. In fact, we've been looking for the Inspector these past two days. Do you know what's happened to him? Your note indicated you had urgent information."

"Sit down and let me explain Constable."

Rowe parked himself in an armchair in the parlour and then promptly stood up again, aware that his coat was dripping wet, he didn't want to mark the furniture.

"Allow me Constable Rowe?" Giles entered and reached out for Rowe's coat who gave it to him with a sheepish nod of thanks. He sat once more, his gangly legs and skinny frame making him look somewhat awkward in the upright armchair. He adjusted his posture; clearly uncomfortable to be in Gunn's company without the presence of the Inspector. He took off his helmet and smoothed his hair, then stroked the line of barely visible blonde fluff above his top lip and cleared his throat.

"So, you were saying sir?" Rowe listened intently as Midnight explained the events of Wednesday evening's ball at the Rainbow Room and their subsequent discovery of the secret club. He admitted to using his powers on Mary and Kim and confessed to a fight in a drug induced state in which he had not meant to kill the man. He told Rowe of his visions of the Inspector, trapped in a cellar somewhere and the urgency of the need to find him as soon as possible.

"We must set out as soon as we have a plan Constable. I understand you will need a statement from me about Kim's death and I'm prepared to go to the station or whatever is needed, I give you my word. But we must find Inspector Gredge first and I know I can help you. I feel like an idiot; had

I not attacked Mary she would've sent a note to Scotland Yard and Arthur would be found."

"We'll talk about your unfortunate experiences another time Mr. Gunn. It is as you say, most urgent that we find the Inspector. What is it you had in mind?"

"This is most unorthodox I know and obviously, Arthur's safety is paramount, but it's imperative that I remain... undiscovered, for want of a better word. I sent for you, Constable Rowe, because I know you to be aware of the capacity in which I assist the Inspector. You understand that, outside of Arthur and your good self, no one else knows what I am."

"I do sir, and it shall remain so. I promise. I can tell the lads we've had an anonymous tip off about the Inspector's whereabouts, get 'em out looking in the cellars of all the places connected with that premises. They'll be glad of something to go on. I admit we've all been standing on our heads over it. We've turned his place over a dozen times in the last two days and followed every possible lead we could think of to no avail. We were starting to think he'd just had one too many pints down the Lamb and Liver and fallen in the bloody river! I would've visited you too sir, only I didn't know you'd seen Inspector Gredge since that day we found the girl in Blackfriars."

"Thank you for keeping my secrets Constable, I appreciate it very much. I cannot afford to be in the limelight. Now, how do you wish to proceed tonight?"

Rowe thought silently for a moment and then said,

"I need to get word to the lads. They can start with Wong's place seeing as he's connected with this Chinese Mary. If there's nothing physical to find we can at least have him brought in for questioning."

"Agreed. Do you need Giles to send for a runner?"

"No, I'd best talk to the Sergeant myself I reckon. Maybe

you could write me an anonymous note or something?" He directed the question to Giles, who nodded. "I can say someone addressed it to me at the station, then we can get the search going."

"I'll do that right away," said Giles and went off to find pen and ink.

"Give me an hour and then I'll meet you back at The Rainbow. It seems too obvious a place to start I know, but there must be something or someone there who can help. She had other staff you say?" Rowe asked Midnight.

"Yes, a doorman and a couple of serving girls plus a group of men and women in *service* so to speak," Rowe raised an eyebrow at Midnight's insinuation. "And I'm fairly sure she had one or two other heavies hidden around the place for protection. I suppose one of them might know of this cellar. What of the body, Constable? It's quite possible my misdeeds have been discovered in the hours I've been here. I doubt I'll be welcomed back."

"True. They won't call us though, that type of business keeps hidden from the authorities. We'll use forced entry if we must. To be honest I could use a few of the lads but that's not an option if we're to keep your involvement a secret."

"What if you were to take me along as a key witness to Arthur's last sighting?"

"How do you mean?"

"There are a hundred witnesses to my attendance at the ball last Wednesday, I was the guest of a Mr. Rudemeister and he knew the Inspector was my companion for the evening. Indeed, I recall Gredge telling him he was there conducting an investigation. You have a legitimate reason for bringing me along, I can say I saw the Inspector ascending the staircase but never saw him return."

"Fine, we can do that. That means I can bring reinforcements should things turn nasty. By the sounds of it we might need them."

Giles returned then and handed Rowe his letter.

"Thank you," Rowe said, taking it. "I'll be off then, and I'll meet you at The Rainbow in one hour, agreed?"

"One hour." They shook hands and Giles handed Rowe his coat. As he turned to leave Midnight called him back, "And Constable? Thank you for keeping my cover. It would not do for anyone else to discover the truth of what I am. I'd rather not become a freak show just yet."

Rowe smiled and tipped his helmet, "I watched you all the years the Inspector has known you, you've helped us many times Mr. Gunn. I don't have a problem with manipulating the truth a little to find the gaffer. He's kept your secrets and so will I."

"The body... I will take responsibility."

"Let's deal with that after we find Gredge." Rowe said kindly. "Priorities."

Rowe left, escorted out by Giles, leaving Midnight alone and anxious. As much as he worried for Arthur and consoled himself with the fact that Kim's death was unintentional and happened whilst he was drugged, he had still killed another human being. He had lost control of his power and caused a death and that was something he could not reconcile. Giles returned to the parlour.

"If you have an hour before you must leave, might I and Mrs. Phillips have a word sir?"

"Of course Giles. What is it?"

Giles came forward and Mrs. Phillips followed.

"Begging your pardon young Master but we should like to discuss Miss Polly."

"Is she calmed? Is she alright?"

"Yes, she's settled. She trusts me more these past few days

and, well..." Mrs. Phillips paused, looking a little uncomfortable.

"Dear Mrs. P. Don't upset yourself. Whatever it is you wish to say, say it."

Clementine still looked unsure, so Giles stepped in,

"Since she woke up, the little miss says she can see things."

"What sort of things?" Midnight sat forward, intrigued.

"She says we look shiny," said Clementine.

"Shiny?"

"Yes sir. Miss says we look like we've been painted in shiny paint. She thought we were angels." This last part made Clementine blush.

"Good grief... of course! It's auras! She can see auras!" Midnight jumped up, suddenly understanding.

"What's that?"

"It's a sort of electromagnetic field that emanates from people, it reflects your moods, thoughts and personality – that type of thing. It's an unusual gift. You say this is a recent thing?"

"Yes sir, when we asked her about it she said it's never happened to her before. Poor lamb thought she was dead and we were angels sent to look after her."

"How interesting. Something must've happened to her while she was in that vegetative state. I thought she'd just put up an emotional barrier but perhaps it was something else."

"There's another thing sir," said Giles. "She has asked us not to let the Devil in again."

"She means me?" Midnight's shoulders drooped.

"We're not sure sir. She said 'the man with two faces'. We don't know what she means. We hoped you might?"

"It could be her attacker I suppose. Two faces? That's curious. Do you think I should try and talk to her again?"

"I don't know sir. No offence but she doesn't seem to take to you too well." Mrs. Phillips shrugged.

"I see."

Mrs. Phillips could tell he was disappointed,

"Let me have another chat with her and see what else I can find out?"

"Of course, yes. Please don't hesitate to come to me if she needs anything?"

"I won't sir." Mrs. Phillips bobbed a quick curtsey and trotted off.

"Giles, I'm going to my study for a little while. I have some time yet before I must journey across town again."

Giles nodded and Midnight made his way past him through the parlour door. He'd had an idea, something that might help Polly.

The Gunn library was vast and highly unusual in that it contained a large number of books on the occult, healing, astrology and magic. It was one of these books on healing that Midnight now opened at his desk in his study. He scanned the chapter that contained information on the healing powers of crystals and semi-precious stones, slapped the desk with his palm when he found what he needed and bounded off to the upper floor where his mother's things were kept.

Josephine Gunn's room had not been touched since the day she died. The only thing that had been replaced was the blood-stained bedlinen from the night Midnight was born. Her clothes, jewellery, books and other possessions remained as they had been on that fateful night. Josiah, Midnight's father, had moved out of their marital chamber the same night and had left instructions that nobody move or dispose of anything. Only the housekeeper had ever been permitted to go in and clean the furniture and lightly dust any surfaces. Of course, Midnight had often sneaked in as a young boy out of stubborn curiosity and the driving need to know his mother. Luckily, he'd never been caught. He'd had a mind to pack it all away and put it in the attic after his father had passed but when it came to it, he found it a comfort to leave it as a tribute to both of them. However, guilt had motivated him to order his father's personal effects to be stored. He didn't want to have to gaze upon anything that reminded him of *that* day.

Midnight found what he was searching for – an intricately carved mahogany box containing his mother's jewels. Inside were several trays that lifted out and all were filled with the baubles and pendants that had once belonged to Josephine. He picked out a silver bracelet with a triangular shaped stone of iridescent blues and greens at the centre. It was Labrodite; a stone known for its protective and healing properties and also for its ability to enhance intuition and strengthen one's own aura. Midnight hoped that wearing the bracelet would reinforce Polly's aura enough to form a protective shield around her. She may feel more in control of what she was seeing in others but mostly, he hoped, it would quell her fear of him. He could only imagine what horror she must see when she looked upon him; his aura would be blackened and spoiled by death and shadow. The Labrodite might let her see his lighter side – the side he presented to the rest of the world.

He found Mrs. Phillips and asked her to accompany him to Polly's room once more.

"Have her put this on," he said and handed her the bracelet. "Let me in when she is wearing it."

"As you please sir." Do you really think it'll help?"

"Only one way to find out Mrs. P."

Clementine knocked gently on the door and called,

"It's only me poppet. Are you awake?" She pushed open the door and went inside, leaving the door ajar a little. Midnight stood closer, ready to enter when called. His heart rate quickened. Why was it so important to him that the girl not be afraid of him? He heard Mrs. Phillips talking softly to her, but the girl seemed to be growing agitated despite efforts to reassure her. Polly was afraid of seeing him again. Disappointment clutched at his heart. He could not stomach the thought of his appearance being so repulsively frightening to a child, especially as he'd taken her under his care. Polly was now his ward, his responsibility. How was he to raise her if she couldn't even stand the sight of him? Mustering his courage, Midnight stepped inside the room. He couldn't wait for Mrs. Phillips to persuade the girl, he had to know now if the stone would work. The chatter stopped the instant he entered. For a moment, the frozen look of fear on Polly's face made his stomach drop – it hadn't worked. Any second now she would begin her screaming and he would be forced to retreat yet again. But then she smiled, a tentative one admittedly but a smile it was and a most welcome sight.

"Hello." Midnight said and returned the smile.

"Um...'ello."

"I'm pleased to see you recovering Miss Polly. My name is..."

"Mista' Midnight, I know."

Midnight's smile broadened. Polly had a broad East-End lilt, a proper little street urchin but all the sweeter for it.

"Do you have a surname Polly? Anyone who might be missing you?"

"Just Polly. Dunno if I had another name, if I did I can't 'member it. Ain't no one gonna be missing me Mista', aside from the rats I shared me bread wiv sometimes, an' that weren't even that often." Polly sat up straight in her bed and looked around her room. "What's this place then? She," she pointed at Clementine, "says it's your house and that you're looking after me now. Is that true? You ain't gonna put me in the workhouse are ya?"

"Well, *just Polly*, Mrs. Phillips has informed you correctly. This is my house and we are looking after you now and no, no workhouse." He smiled kindly, she was a jaunty little thing.

"You promise? 'Cos I'd rather be selling me matches again than go in the workhouse. Them that goes there don't come out."

"I promise." You can stay with us as long as you are happy to."

"S'at mean I live here now then?" Her eager eyes lit up.

"Yes, if that's what you want?"

Polly narrowed her eyes and looked around again, she ran her little pink hand over the smooth cotton sheet and peered back at Midnight.

"I might. If I likes the look of the place. 'Appen I might take a wander around and then decide eh?"

"I'd be delighted to show you the house Miss Polly but perhaps when you're a little stronger?" Midnight lowered his voice to a conspiratorial whisper. "By the look on Mrs. Phillips face she'd skin me alive if I got you out of bed just yet." This last statement elicited an animated giggle from the girl. Midnight thought it the most delightful sound he'd ever heard. His heart lightened and for once he forgot the shadows and basked in the positive energy that radiated from his new charge. A knock at the door broke the spell and Giles entered.

"Forgive the interruption sir but I believe you must leave now to go and meet the Constable."

"Yes, I must. Thank you, Giles." Giles nodded and retreated, Midnight turned his attention back to Polly. "I have to go now, young lady, but I leave you in the very capable hands of Mrs. Phillips. I promise to give you the grand tour as soon as you're up and about. And Polly, I must ask that you keep the bracelet on. It will help you recover."

"Why? Is it magic?" She asked, wide-eyed.

Midnight chuckled.

"You could say that. It will make you feel better faster. It belonged to my mother, so you must take good care of it, alright?"

"Alright Mista' Midnight," Polly replied too busy gazing in wonder at her new magical jewel to pay him much mind anymore. Mrs. Phillips arose and followed him from the bedroom.

"Take care of her Mrs. P. Make sure she keeps the bracelet on. I'll take it to a jeweller after we find Inspector Gredge and have something made to fit her. But, for now it should help her."

"She's in good hands Sir. You just make sure to take care of yourself and return soon with the Inspector. Leave the rest to me and Mr. Morgan."

"Thank you. I'll return as soon as I can."

"God's speed sir."

"I may need more than that I fear."

14

GREDGE

I t was the slow, rhythmic echo of dripping of water that eventually roused him, or it could've been the smell – dank and rotten. It assaulted his nostrils and caused him a fit of spontaneous hacking coughs. Gredge sat up too quickly and immediately regretted it. His head span and he felt burning bile rise in his throat. He retched and tried to raise himself onto his knees but it was so dark, for a second he couldn't tell which way was up. It was only the cold hardness of stone under his hands that brought him back from the brink of panic. He'd never been good in dark places, especially since he knew the things that lay in wait amongst the shadows.

Breathe!

Still on all fours, Arthur forced himself to focus.

That's it... in and out, in and out. I'm alive... breathe... stop fucking panicking man!

When he'd slowed his breathing to something relatively normal and stopped feeling sick, Arthur sat back on his heels, squeezed his eyes tight shut then opened them. It was pitch black.

Stop it! There's nothing to be afraid of you idiot.

He slapped his own face hard. The sound echoed and the hairs on the back of his neck rose.

Where in Christ's name am I?

His mind remained foggy. He shook his head and then wished he hadn't as he retched again.

Gunn, club, he was... drinking and then... Kim! Bastard hit me! Where the hell am I then? Fuck... alive... thank God. Need to get out! Shit! Think... come on Arthur, you're a copper... think!

His head was pounding, tentatively he reached up and felt the tender lump on his skull.

Bastard.

Gredge wondered how long he had been in whatever hole he now found himself in. Clearly Gunn's plan hadn't worked and he wondered what fate had befallen his friend. The plinking of water triggered his sudden, raging thirst. Along with a terrible sense of foreboding; like the ticking of a clock marking the passing of time.

Crawling on all fours he scuttled to his left, fumbling around in the blackness, his hands and knees trailing through cold slime and organic matter that he couldn't allow himself to think on for fear of what it might be. Gredge reached out blindly, hoping his fingers may grasp something, anything that may give him either a drink or some idea of where he was. He felt empty air.

Keep moving till you find a wall, idiot!

When he finally felt brick his relief was palpable. Now he could navigate his prison and perhaps find a way out.

There must be a door. Stairs, anything... move slowly... keep moving. Listen. Focus.

A shuffling noise caused his head to swing to the right,

"Who's there? Gunn, is that you?" His voice hoarse, his throat dry and sore, his demands were lost to the dark. The high-pitched squeak quelled his fear somewhat.

Just a rat... fucking hate rats.

Fumbling his way along the brick wall, his feet shuffled forwards inch by inch, hoping to find something other than the empty dark. He cursed loudly when his right foot kicked something heavy. He kicked it again to ascertain what it might be. The dull thud that came back at him suggested something like a rolled-up rug and he bent to investigate. At this point – thirsty, filthy and cold – a rug would be a gratifying find. At least he'd have something other than wet stone to sit on. Arthur let out a sigh of relief as his hands touched the unmistakable texture of tough, woven fabric. He felt around for the rug's edge and gave it a tug but it did not unravel.

Stuck.

He reached over the large roll to see what might be blocking it. There was nothing but empty space. He grabbed a firmer hold and heaved upwards. The rug rolled reluctantly, accompanied by a distinct 'thub-dub' indicating that something else had rolled out of it. Years of experience in the force told him this could not be a good sound. This was a body.

Just for a second he forgot to breathe, he forgot his police training and felt a stab of fear in his gut. He was alone in a dark, underground hovel with a corpse. It was then he wondered if he himself had been thrown into this horror pit to die.

Check if they're dead. Might not be. Two heads are better than one. Might be able to help them.

Hesitantly, Arthur reached out and skimmed his hand over the body until he found the neck. The skin was ice and he knew there was no need to check for a pulse. He couldn't see the corpse but by the feel of it she was female. She felt stiff and he didn't think she had begun to putrefy but it was freezing in this hole, which he knew could affect the decomposition rate. The smell was a different matter; old blood, stale urine and faeces mingled to produce a stench so overpowering it made his eyes water. Arthur slung the rug back over the dead woman and backed away. Determined to find an exit, he shuffled along the wall in the opposite direction. He found the bottom step of a wooden staircase and scrambled up it on his hands and knees. The heavy door at the top was locked but he banged hard on it anyway.

"Hello? Can anyone hear me? I'm trapped! My name is Inspector Arthur Gredge of Scotland Yard. If you can hear me please help!" He put his ear to the door and listened; nothing but his own pounding heartbeat answered him.

Damn!

He tried the handle again. It rattled but didn't shift.

Break it down. Find something.

Scurrying back down into the room, Arthur searched blindly for something solid which might serve to break the door. After what seemed an age, for he had no concept of time down here, he gave up, his frustration evident in his sweaty underarms, and the tugging of his moustache. It was clear to him that if someone didn't find him soon, he was a goner. He must have faith that Gunn got away from The Rainbow and was searching for him. He was an inspector at Scotland Yard dammit! Somebody must have noticed his absence? But what if they hadn't? What if Gunn had been killed? He'd been drugged after all – how that might have affected his powers? What if he'd not even been down a single day? He'd have to suffer the horror of slowly starving to death... probably like the woman in the rug!

I'd have been better off unconscious. Least I wouldn't know I was dying...

oh stop it!

"Yearghh! Come on Gunn! Where are you?" His shouts reverberated off the walls, mocking him, emphasizing his solitude. It was at that moment he stepped back and knocked something metal. A sloshing wet sound mingled with the metallic noise and he noticed the dripping had stopped. Bending, his fingers found the object. It was a bucket. A bucket that had been filled with water and was now laid empty on its side, its contents spilled.

Fuck!

There was nothing to be done except put it back and wait. Arthur sat heavily down on the wooden stairs, his thirst ever more pressing, wondering just how long it would take for the slow dripping to provide him with a drink.

15

GUESTS AND GHOSTS

The clink of the bell was an unpleasant sound. It summoned him from a place he did not want to leave; lost in his thoughts and the failure, thus far, to find his friend. Midnight knew Arthur did not have much time left, he might even be dead already. They had searched; him, Rowe, the men from Southwark and the Metropolitan Police, they'd scoured the Rainbow rooms and the club. They'd visited all the opium dens, the rookeries and the brothels to no avail. The worst of it was, Midnight had not been able to use his powers on Chinese Mary again because she was gone. The first place they had looked was the Rainbow. Gunn had not been keen to revisit knowing what he'd left behind – Kim's corpse – but the body had gone and so had Mary and all her staff. They had vanished and left behind no records or documents that appeared useful. The Rainbow was a ghost ship, one unwilling to give up her secrets.

The next place they had gone was Wong's tea shop. Wong, of course, denied all knowledge of Mary and the Rainbow but Midnight already knew he was lying, he hadn't needed to use his senses for that. He felt no guilt in telling Wong of his previous encounter with his money-runner, the father of five who collected the takings from all of Wong's undeclared businesses. Wong would no doubt fire the poor man if not worse, but finding Arthur was paramount and Midnight could not afford to let any sympathies for the clerk and his family get in the way of this investigation, not now. If indeed the clerk had been telling the truth, Midnight eased his conscience by promising himself to properly compensate the man for losing his job once Arthur was found... dead or alive. Rowe had asked Wong if he knew where Mary was or of any acquaintances in the city she might run to and he'd answered no. His answer had been truthful to a point, but Midnight could sense something seemed a little off; Wong was hiding something, he just couldn't put his finger on it.

For two days, they had searched and come up with nothing but a half-truth and a box of old papers and junk that Rowe told him held nothing of value. Midnight had asked if he might go through them himself just in case, and this is what he now sat in his cellar room doing. The bell jangled again, this time a little more demanding. He sighed and made his way out of the room and up the steps to answer the summons. Giles met him in the library,

"Apologies sir, but Mrs. Phillips is having a fit and has insisted I come and bring you."

"Are they here then?"

"They are. I am to escort you to the front door to greet our new guests at the request of..."

"Mrs. Phillips. I know," he sighed. "Come along then, best not keep everybody waiting. Is everything in order?" They chatted as they walked together.

"It is sir. Their rooms are in the same wing as Miss Polly's, and the nurse's room too."

"And she will arrive when, exactly?"

"On the morrow. Miss Annabelle Carstairs. She came highly recommended and seems like a very pleasant and capable woman."

"Excellent Giles, I'm sure she will do nicely. I can trust you and Mrs. Phillips to have good judgement in such matters."

"Thank you, sir."

They came into the entrance hall to find Mrs. Phillips flapping and fussing like a mother hen as two men in the staff uniforms of the All Souls Asylum escorted Billy Bromley and Miss Sally into the house.

"Giles, would you mind?" Midnight gestured toward Mr. Bromley, who was getting on in years and was struggling to negotiate the front door steps. Giles held up Mr. Bromley from the right as the asylum employee held him up from the left.

"That's right Billy, lift your foot now, step up." Midnight noticed that Billy automatically did as the employee instructed but there was no emotional response, he merely stared blankly into the distance. It struck him once again how strangely *empty* these victims appeared. It was as if they'd had the life sucked from them and...

"That's it!" Midnight declared, much to the surprise of those around him.

"Sir?"

"Giles! I know what's wrong with them! Well, at least I have a theory. Come let's get them settled, then I can see if I am correct." One of the uniformed men handed him some papers to sign, which Midnight did hurriedly, eager to test his theory.

"All yours now Mr. Gunn. There's no luggage, they didn't have none."

"Thank you," Midnight handed one copy of the papers back to the man. "Please inform Mr. Hawksmith his cheque will be delivered in due course." The man took the papers, nodded and left. Midnight turned to Mrs. Phillips and Giles who now held onto Miss Sally and Billy respectively.

"I shall escort Mr. Bromley, Giles if you'd be so kind as to help Mrs. P with the young lady?"

When they had settled both patients into their rooms Midnight drew Mrs. Phillips aside.

"I have a theory and I think I can prove it, but I will need Miss Polly's help. Do you think her well enough?"

"Depends what you have in mind I suppose Sir? What is it you require her to do exactly?"

"Just visit our new guests and look at them, that's all."

"Look at 'em?"

"That's all, I promise. Is she well enough to walk? I will carry her if not."

Mrs. Phillips chuckled.

"Happen she'll be glad of the chance to get out of bed and have a little wander, she's been begging to for the last two days."

Midnight grinned and followed his housekeeper to Polly's room.

The girl was, as Mrs. Phillips predicted, more than happy to oblige. Polly scrambled eagerly from her bed and into her slippers and dressing gown. Midnight waited at the door, checking she had the Labrodite bracelet on before he stepped inside. She greeted him with a beaming smile and he could not help but return it. She surprised him more when he felt her right hand slip into his as they walked the corridor together. He heard a sniffle behind him and turned his head to catch Mrs. Phillips dabbing at her eyes with a handkerchief. He thought on how oddly satisfying it felt to have a child in his household after so many years of isolation. Now he had two other guests in his home that he was responsible for. Opening his house to strangers was something he would've never considered a few months ago. He'd worked dozens of cases alongside Gredge, yet none had affected him like this. Glancing at Polly, skipping beside him, he realized it was because of her; she had changed his heart. He wasn't quite ready to enter society; his secret must remain a secret for all time, but Midnight was beginning to see the benefits of having a young soul such as Miss Polly in his life.

They stopped outside Sally's room and Midnight faced Polly.

"Are you ready child?"

"Mm-hmm," she nodded.

"I will need you to remove your bracelet Polly." The girl's expression changed to one of fear and he quickly reassured her. "Only for a moment and you must not look at me. Do you understand? Look only at the woman in this room and tell me what you see. Mrs. Phillips will hand you back your bracelet before you come out."

"Alright Mista Midnight."

"Mrs. Phillips, if you would?"

"Yes Sir. Come now Polly. We shall enter together and say hello to our guest." They went through the door together and then the housekeeper returned alone with Polly's bracelet. Midnight called through the heavy oak door,

"Don't be afraid Polly. Miss Sally is sick just like you were and we need to help her. I need you to tell me what you see when you look at Miss Sally." There was a moment of silence and then,

"Nuffink. I don't see nuffink."

"Are you looking right at Miss Sally, Polly?"

"Yeah course, like you told me to but... she ain't shiny like you or Missus P and Mista Morgan is."

Midnight's fears were confirmed.

"Do you see any colours at all Polly? Grey or black even?"

"Nah, nuffink."

"Good girl, Mrs. Phillips will bring your bracelet. Put it on before we visit Mr. Bromley."

Clementine returned to Polly and a thought occurred to him.

"Polly, do you have it on?"

"Yes Mista."

"Just look at her again. Do you see anything now?" An agonizing silence prevailed as he waited for some response, "Polly? Do you see anything?"

"Um... sort of. She still ain't shiny but there's not nuffink anymore."

"Can you describe it to me?"

"Um... well, it's a kind of a nuffink but one I can see."

"Any colour?"

"Nah, it's strange Mista' Midnight. It's sort of like a Miss Sally-shaped hole I suppose, only I can see it... bit like looking through a window. Yeah that's it, a window!"

"You've done well child. You can come out now."

Polly exited the door with a sad smile.

"Is that what I looked like?"

Midnight kneeled and tugged one of her dark curls,

"Absolutely not, you were like Brier-Rose, only very much prettier."

"Who's she?"

"A sleeping princess. I'll read you her story one day."

"Ain't nobody ever read me a story before. Will I like it?"

"I shall read you many stories and you will love them all I'm sure," he smiled. "Are you ready to visit Mr. Bromley?"

Polly nodded and the three of them headed down the corridor to Billy's room. Mrs. Phillips knocked and went in first then Polly followed.

"Same again please Polly, look both with and without the bracelet. What do you see?"

"He's the same as the other lady, Mista' Midnight."

"Thank you, child."

"Did I do good?" Polly asked when she stood in front of him again.

"You were perfect. You should go back to your room and rest now. Mrs. Phillips will bring you refreshments."

"Will you read me that story, about the princess?" she asked, a hopeful glint in her eyes.

"Later perhaps, at bedtime. I must talk with Mr. Morgan now and then I must continue my efforts to find my friend."

"Oh...alright then." Her face fell in disappointment. "You promise?"

"I promise. Now go with Mrs. Phillips."

Polly turned to the housekeeper and asked,

"What time is bedtime?"

"Supper is at half past six Miss, then bedtime at seven."

"I'll see you at seven then Mista'," she declared and Midnight chuckled.

"Seven o'clock sharp!" he replied, winking at a smiling Mrs. Phillips as she took the girl back to her room.

Midnight went to find Giles and asked him to send word to Constable Rowe that he had discovered what ailed the remaining Spring-Heeled Jack victims and to come visit as soon as he could.

"Might I ask what it is you've discovered sir? It may help in the care of our two patients when nurse Carstairs arrives tomorrow."

"I will tell you Giles, but it will not aid us in caring for these two poor unfortunates, not in any way."

"It is that bad sir?"

"It is. Let us say that Jack has done them no favours in

leaving his victims alive. At this stage, they would have been better off dead."

Giles looked shocked,

"But... Miss Polly?"

"Polly was fortunate enough not to have suffered the same fate. She merely blocked her mind from whatever it was that happened to her that night. I must conclude that her attacker somehow got disturbed and did not get what he came for."

"And what was that?"

"Her soul, Giles. Spring-Heeled Jack is harvesting souls."

16

POLLY PEEPS

Midnight waited impatiently in his library for Constable Rowe. He'd brought the box of papers from the Rainbow with him and riffled though it piece by piece looking for anything that might indicate where Mary had gone. There were receipts for alcohol, furniture, and other such domestic items, but nothing to tie her to Wong or any suggestion of another premises anywhere in London. He banged his fist on the desk and swore. If only he hadn't killed Kim, he could perhaps have probed his mind and discovered the truth of Arthur's disappearance. In his frustration, Midnight pushed the box away from him and it toppled over onto the floor.

"Bathsheba's backside!" He cursed and stomped around the desk to gather the fallen papers. A giggle and a flash of white caught his eye. "Aren't you supposed to be in bed little Miss Peeper? It's impolite to spy on people you know."

Polly stepped out boldly and stood defiant in her white cotton nightdress and slippers.

"I ain't spying! I was just having a wander is all. You promised me a story."

Midnight sat back on his heels and looked at the grandfather clock in the corner.

"Is it seven o'clock yet Miss Peeps?"

"I dunno... I can't tell time, can I." She shrugged, and Midnight struggled to suppress a smile.

"It's barely six, young lady, which means you've yet to have supper. Mrs. Phillips will have a fit if she finds you missing from your room. As for not being able to tell time...well, we shall have to remedy that. We shall find you a governess once you are up to it."

"You don't half speak funny Mista'." Polly observed

"And you are far too brazen for your own good," he quipped back.

"What's that mean then?"

"It means that if you want a bedtime story then you had better hop over here and help me pick up this mess."

"That's not what it means!"

"Indeed, it is not but you won't find out the truth unless you help me."

Polly stood with her hands behind her back swinging her shoulders from side to side, observing him through narrowed eyes. He raised his eyebrows questioningly at her.

"I can tell you're only joking you know."

"Oh, you can? How can you be so sure Miss Peeps?"

"It's your colours, they're all swirly. I seen it on Missus P. and Mista' Morgan too. When they're happy their shines go all swirly."

Midnight panicked a little.

"Polly, are you wearing your bracelet?"

She dangled her right arm in front of her to display the jewel.

"Course I am. It makes 'em brighter. It's nicer too 'cause then I can't see the other bits."

"What other bits?"

"The dark," she stated, "and your face don't look dead anymore."

He was stunned by her second statement. He'd expected she could see his dark side, that's why she'd screamed in fear of him before, but he was baffled by what she said about his face.

"How did my face look dead? You mean it looked dark?"

"Nah, you looked proper dead... only half of it, mind you." She screwed up her face in thought, struggling to articulate her meaning. "It was like you had two faces, one was you and the other was bones... I thought you was death come to get me."

"Oh child, I am sorry to have frightened you so." He understood her initial fear of him fully now; she had first thought Clementine and Giles to be angels, they were 'shiny', and he must have looked monstrous in comparison. He'd had no idea his darkness had a face! That was certainly a revelation. "And you do not fear me now?"

Polly shook her head making her curls bounce.

"Mm-mm. Mista' Morgan said you was special, a kind of angel that scares away bad people. I 'spect you would scare 'em if they seen that mush too. No offence mind."

"None taken." Midnight could not help but marvel at the bravery and fortitude of the little urchin that, for all intents and purposes, was his child now. He gestured for her to come to him. "Miss Polly Peeps, you see more than anyone realizes and I think that will see you in good stead as you grow." He tugged playfully on her curls again. "Mr. Morgan is very kind to explain things to you. One day soon I will tell you all about me and then you will never have to be afraid, ever again." And then Polly did the most extraordinary thing he had ever encountered; she threw her arms around his neck and hugged him. It took him a few seconds to respond, he was so taken aback by the gesture. Her face was tucked into the crook of his neck, buried beneath her arms that held him so tightly. The lights in the library flared suddenly, filling the room with a glorious glow. Midnight had never seen his light powers flourish thus. His dark side had always dominated and he realized the surge was fuelled by an increasing regard for the child. He responded and wrapped her up in a gentle embrace.

"Does this mean you'll help me tidy up this mess then?"

She giggled and her head popped up to meet his gaze

"Only if you read me the princess story like you promised."

"You are a wily one, aren't you? It's a deal Miss Peeps."

Polly let him go and held out her left arm, its hand missing.

"Bump stumps on it?"

He was shocked how she could be so blasé about her disability and it must have shown on his face because Polly burst into a fit of giggles,

"Ha ha! I got you good!" She thumped him on the chest with her arm, "Don't worry Mista', I get everyone wiv that one." Her ceaseless giggling was contagious and soon he found himself chuckling alongside her.

They had almost cleared the mess of papers when her cheerful demeanour changed suddenly. Polly stood frozen to the spot, staring at a tatty show poster of some sort on the floor.

"What is it child? What's wrong?" Midnight scooped up the poster, it was a flyer for a mesmerist show. He read it out loud.

"An evening of mesmerism, magic and mime with Hemlock Nightingale, live at the Old Vic Theatre, every Monday to Friday." A cold feeling settled in his gut. "Nightingale... Polly, do you recognize this man?" The poster had a pen-and-ink drawing of a showman in the centre, dressed in striped trousers and dark tailcoat with a curled moustache and pointed beard. Polly gulped and nodded her head.

"He's... he's the devil Mista' Midnight. Please don't let him get me." Her bottom lip began to tremble and Midnight scooped her into his arms.

"I won't Polly. I won't let him hurt you again."

He stood up and carried her from the Library, shouting to Giles as he ascended the stairs. The butler came running.

"Giles, we cannot afford to wait for Constable Rowe. Tell Mrs. Phillips she must attended to Miss Polly immediately and she must tell Rowe to meet us at The Old Vic theatre in Southwark. It's on the corner of New Cut and Oakley Street. Hurry!" Giles didn't reply. He sensed the urgency in his master's voice and went to find the housekeeper. Meanwhile, Midnight carried the girl upstairs and tucked her up in her bed.

"Polly, promise me you will stay in your room until I return?"

The girl nodded and scooted down further under her sheets.

"Are you going to find him?"

"I am, and I'm going to make him go away."

"He's a devil Mista'. He fools people, just like he fooled Mr. Hawksmith."

And suddenly another piece of the puzzle fell into place.

"The mime artist..." He whispered to himself. Spring-Heeled Jack had been right there under their noses that day at the asylum.

"I knew it was him, I could feel it. Only I couldn't say nuffink 'cause me mind wouldn't work properly. I was trying to scream but nuffink came out. You will catch him won't you Mista'?"

"I'll catch him Polly, I promise. I'm sorry about the bedtime story."

"Read it when you come back?" she pleaded

"I'll ask Mrs. Phillips to bring it up from the library so you can have it ready for me." This seemed to please her, perhaps help reassure her that he was coming back. "I have to go now sweetheart. Be good and do as Mrs. Phillips instructs."

Midnight met Giles in the entrance hall who already had on his coat and hat. He handed his master his outdoor attire and when Midnight had finished buttoning up his coat, Giles handed him his selenite pendant.

"It seems as though the situation called for it."

"Thank you, Giles. Yes, I'm afraid we're going to need all the help we can get this night."

"Then I am glad to inform you sir that I brought a lucky charm of my own." Giles patted a lump in his pocket that seemed to Midnight distinctly pistol-shaped.

"That may indeed come in useful tonight. Be careful," he added.

Mrs. Phillips had her instructions for the constable and she locked the door behind them to await Rowe's arrival. They hailed a hansom cab and once settled, Midnight began to explain his discovery to Giles.

"I do not know what we face this evening and although I am sure Hemlock Nightingale is but an ordinary human being, I am equally sure there is more to him than meets the eye. I cannot explain how he is harvesting souls, or how he is able to make such extraordinary leaps, the eyewitness accounts of demonic eyes, none of that. But I do know *why*. Father had many books at home on the occult. Because of what I am he sought to find answers – solutions – to my abilities, so he could help me lead a normal life. After his death..."

Midnight faltered. "After his death, there was not much else for a solitary freak like me to do other than read. There is only one reason that I can think of why Hemlock would want to reap souls and I pray, to whatever deity hears my plea, that he does not succeed."

17

THE OLD VIC

They stood on the stone steps of the Old Vic between the two grand columns and peered through the glass panes of the entrance doors. All was in darkness. It was Monday evening, so the place should have been heaving with theatre-goers expecting to see Hemlock's show. But a hastily pasted sign on the door announced that tonight's show had been cancelled due to unforeseen circumstances.

"There's no one here Giles. We are going to have to break in."

"Then perhaps we should wait for the police?"

"No time! We need to catch this bastard now. He must know where Mary is. It all fits. Remember Bessie Green, the girl who escaped attack? Her description in the news report mentioned a 'black-tongued creature'; consistent opium use turns teeth and tongues black. We found the show poster in the box of papers from the Rainbow, which suggests Hemlock was a client. Mary said she made it her business to know everything worth knowing about her clients. She made a lot of money for Wong in that club. There's no chance she'd disappear and not let her clientele know where she would be relocating to *and* I could tell Wong was holding something back when we asked about his other businesses. This theatre closed in 1856 and it has never been announced who took over the lease and yet here we have a mesmerist show playing five days a week! There *has* to be a connection between Hemlock, Mary and Wong and I believe this theatre is the key." Midnight stopped his ranting at the sound of breaking glass and stared at Giles who had just used the butt of his pistol to smash the window. Giles reached through the broken pane and unbolted the door.

"After you, sir. As you said, let's get this blackguard."

They stepped through the grand entrance into the foyer. The gas lights were off and the place was in total darkness. Shadows pulsed in his presence; they were with him always and this time there was no light source to manipulate.

"I need light, do you have any Matches?"

"No sir, but might I suggest the kiosk?"

"Ah! Yes, of course they would have some." He scrambled over to the kiosk and fumbled around on the shelves till he heard the rattle of matchboxes. Pulling out a box he lit one of the matches and immediately thought of Polly. The match flared brighter and he focused on its glow, bringing its energy towards him he blended it with his own, and the flame grew bigger until he held a swirling ball of flame in his palm. He pocketed the box of matches. The foyer lit up enough for them to make out their surroundings and locate the signs that said, 'Stalls' and 'Dress Circle'.

"Which way sir?"

"Stalls. He would be backstage in the dressing rooms I think? We'll make our way to the stage via the stalls and go backstage from there. Stay close to the wall, don't go down the middle aisle, we need to stay hidden from view and the balconies will mask us hopefully."

The Old Vic auditorium was beautiful, not as magnificent as some of the West End theatres, but Midnight could see past the peeling paint, tatty seats and tobacco stains to what it must have looked like in its heyday. It had closed some four years ago but he hadn't known it had reopened and it was clear that the new owners had not seen fit to refurbish it. Mesmerism and magic shows were cheap sensationalism in his eyes; putting someone in a trance to perform tricks for the cheering crowds. Some mesmerists claimed to be mediums, he knew the veil beyond death was real enough but rarely did one find a medium who could truly communicate with the dead. It was all just showmanship and entertainment. A flashback of the mime artist in the asylum, wagging his finger at him for the intrusion on his performance, caused the ball of flame to stutter in his anger and the shadows called to him. If he had only known then, he could have caught him and poor Polly would... he stopped short.

"Polly!"

"What is it sir?" Giles whispered.

"The day I found Polly at the asylum, *he* was there! He was putting on a skit for the inmates. But what are the chances, Giles? No, that's too much of a coincidence. He was there for Polly. He came back for her!"

"But why sir? Surely there are a hundred other waifs on the streets he could've taken? Why go to the trouble of tracking down one child?

"I don't know Giles but I'm sure of it. He wanted Polly." He began making his way toward the stage once more, hugging the wall and dimming the flames in his hand.

"If that is the case sir, then we must prevail this evening and find him."

"Agreed," replied Midnight as he clambered up the set of wooden steps to the side of the stage. There were various contraptions and props set upon the boards in readiness for the next show.

"Here. The sign says the dressing rooms are this way."

They made their way as stealthily as they could, down a flight of stone steps towards the dressing rooms. Giles had his pistol ready. Something about the cold corridor jogged Midnight's memory. The dressing room doors were locked so they went deeper into the belly of the building and that's when it hit him.

"Arthur's here! I remember this from Mary's memory. This is the corridor they took him down." A renewed urgency in his step, Midnight hurried to the end where he now knew a bolted door to the cellar was. He sent the ball of flame to the ceiling to light the doorway. It was heavy and bolted just like he recalled. Banging loudly with his fists he shouted for his friend.

"Arthur? Arthur Gredge, are you down there?"

"Sir, the noise?"

"No time! He could be dead already! Stand guard while I break it down."

"No need sir, stand aside." Midnight didn't understand until he saw Giles point the pistol at the padlock. Giles aimed and fired. The blast resounded loudly in the narrow stone corridor but the lock pinged open and Midnight shoved the door aside. He sent the ball of flame ahead to light the way as they descended.

"Arthur? Where are you?" The ball of flame flickered and Midnight had to force back the shadows that sensed his agitation. He could hardly see, even with the flames but he was too distracted finding Arthur to make them brighter. "Help me Giles! He *must* be here."

In his haste to help, Giles kicked over a metal bucket and water sloshed everywhere. The cellar was huge and reeked like the bowels of Hell. Scattered around were various old props covered in thick layers of dust, they clearly had not been used in years.

"Over there! Sir, look!" Giles pointed to the far corner where a pale human hand was just visible behind a piece of painted scenery board. They ran towards it. Midnight flung back the stained rug that covered the rest of the body, his heart thumping. Were they too late? Had Arthur perished?

"It's Mary!" He gaped at the unmoving body of Chinese Mary and hope of finding his friend alive left him. "I was so sure he was here. I know he was. It's the same place I saw in... her head. Watch the door Giles!" Crouching over her body, Midnight summoned the shadows and the light from the flames was snuffed out. His sense of urgency to find Arthur, staved off the fear that he might lose control again. He focused hard on the task at hand.

Her memories came slower than before. He removed the remnants of the energy he'd left inside her head that day at The Rainbow, but they were still hard to decipher. The state of the corpse often dictated the quality of his visions and her corpse must be two or three days old but he could still make out the corridor, the door and Kim throwing Gredge into the abyss. He had been right, this was the place. He pushed harder, eager to see more memories in the days preceding Arthur's capture. A man was talking, he concentrated harder on the vision and it became clearer.

"I'm warning you to stay out of it. It's none of your business!"

"When you involve my premises, it is! Wong will not be happy. I will have to revoke your membership."

"Go ahead. You think I care about a silly club? It served a purpose, that is all."

Midnight was viewing the scene through Mary's eyes. He saw her walk over to her desk and sit down. Then, he got his

first good look at Hemlock Nightingale. Without the grease-
paint and gaudy costume he'd worn at the asylum, he was the
epitome of a gentleman. His way of speaking, dapper attire,
pointed beard and perfectly curled moustache, all screamed
money. The man was clearly educated. It made no sense that
such a person would choose a career in low-end entertainment... unless it gave him easy access to his prey? After all,
who noticed when the poor of London went missing? It was
only the discovery of the murdered Emeline Rowbotham – the
daughter of a wealthy family – that had prompted a full-scale
investigation into the attacks.

Midnight probed further.

*"Oh Mr. 'Nightingale', you have no idea what I am capable of
and it would do you well to heed my warning. I make it my business to know everything worth knowing about my clientele." She
rose from her seat and propped her hands on the desk. "For instance;
I know Hemlock Nightingale is not your real name. I know you
were discredited and removed from the British Medical Association
five years ago when..." the vision went black and then jumped
forward in time to the very moment of her death – an enraged,
laughing Hemlock lunging forward, a paperweight in his hand.
Mary, frightened and confused.*

"Please, Sir? No! What are you doing?

"Loose ends my dear, I told you to stay out of it!"

"Nightingale killed her," Midnight told Giles. "She knew
things about him he obviously didn't want known, and when
she discovered Miss Rowbotham was dead, she threatened to
expose him. Only the blackguard didn't know I had meddled
with her memory. He had no reason to kill her."

"But, how did this woman learn that this man Nightingale
was the killer?"

"I'm not sure yet but there has to be a connection. Mary
said something about Nightingale being discredited from the

British Medical Association. Miss Rowbotham had psychiatric issues. Mary also said he was using an alias. Giles, we need to get hold of Rowe and find out who, in the last five years, has been struck from the list of registered doctors or psychiatrists, it may give us another lead."

A noise from the exterior corridor caught their attention. Giles cocked his pistol, the action sounded too loud in the silent dark. Midnight listened, he heard measured footsteps, more than one set, and clipped urgent mutterings. The lack of light prevented him from signalling Giles, so he risked a whisper and urged his companion to hold steady in case it was theatre staff. Using the shadows, he focused on sensing the emotions of the people coming down the corridor. He could almost taste their anticipation and unease, but something told him they were benevolent in purpose. He whispered to Giles to lower his gun and the butler did so reluctantly.

"Constable Rowe, is that you?"

The footsteps halted,

"Gunn? How... how did you know?" Rowe answered not attempting to hide the surprise and relief in his voice.

"Let us call it practice, shall we?"

Rowe and two other policemen appeared in the cellar doorway with a lantern, filling the cellar with a welcome light.

"Well, did you find anything?" Rowe asked, peering into the gloom.

"The body of Chinese Mary but naught else. Nightingale isn't here but there's something you need to know. Inspector Gredge was here, I am sure of it."

"Gredge? Where is he now?"

"I don't know but I think we need to contact the British Medical Association..."

"Mr. Gunn, you can tell me on the way."

"On the way where?"

"Your house sir. There's been an... incident, and you need to go home. We came here to find you. Your housekeeper told us where you'd gone."

"What's happened? It there something wrong with Miss Sally or Mr. Bromley, have they taken ill?"

Rowe shook his head and looked very uncomfortable.

"Not ill... they're dead. Murdered, in fact... in your house."

Midnight felt the cold creep into his chest and extend its crushing hand to his throat as it tightened with dread. He swallowed hard and forced the next word from his mouth.

"Polly?"

"Missing Sir, we think she's been taken."

18

ODE TO A NIGHTINGALE

"**S**HOW ME the note."

Rowe passed Midnight a piece of paper. "It's a poem Sir, that's all he left behind."

Midnight read it.

> "My heart aches, and a drowsy numbness pains
> My sense, as though of hemlock I had drunk,
> Or emptied some dull opiate to the drains
> One minute past, and Lethe-wards had sunk:
> 'Tis not through envy of thy happy lot,
> But being too happy in thine happiness, —
> That thou, light-winged Dryad of the trees
> In some melodious plot
> Of beechen green, and shadows numberless,
> Singest of summer in full-throated ease."

He paused and flipped the paper over.

"Where's the rest?"

"The rest?"

"The rest of the poem."

Constable Rowe started back blankly.

"It's John Keats 'Ode to a Nightingale' but this is only the first stanza, where's the rest?" he demanded.

"There is none sir, that's all he left."

"That bastard is taunting us! Giles?"

"Yes sir?"

"Fetch me the Keats collection. Aisle two, third shelf along, second shelf down."

Giles gave a short nod and scurried off to the library. Rowe stepped to Midnight's side and read the poem.

"What is it you're thinking?"

"It's a message."

"Well what does it mean?"

"I don't know yet, but I think it's for me. He has Gredge, I know it, and Polly. He killed Sally and Billy because he didn't need them and he knew it would keep the police busy. It's me he wants and he's using Arthur and Polly to draw me out. This," he held up the poem, "is a message for me and I must decipher it."

Constable Rowe shook his head,

"I ain't got no mind for poetry. I have to process these murders. The commissioner wants a report as soon as possible. I have yours and your housekeeper's statements, not much else I can do right now but wait here for the resurrection men to come and collect the bodies."

"Of course, thank you constable. I must go and check on poor Clementine again before I begin. She has suffered such trauma this night."

"She took quite a blow to the bonce, your housekeeper."

Midnight felt a surge of anger course through him, making the shadows twitch excitedly. He quickly suppressed it. It wouldn't do to let that side of him show with a house full of strangers, especially policemen. Constable Rowe was familiar with him in the sense that he knew him as Gredge's preferred case consultant, and they had met several times but Midnight had been careful never to show the full extent of his powers to anyone, even Gredge.

Midnight found Mrs. Phillips upstairs in Polly's room. She sat on the bed with her back to the door, weeping. She turned when she heard him enter.

"Oh, your Lordship! Forgive me? It's all my fault!"

"Calm yourself dear Mrs. P. None of this is your fault. Who was to know that maniac would be watching the house? I should have been more vigilant and not left you alone. I should have waited for Rowe to arrive before Giles and I went out. There are a lot of things I should have done." He thought back to the mime artist at the asylum; to Chinese Mary, whose mind he'd made so addled she could not defend herself against Nightingale; Kim, who had died by his hand... Polly, whom he'd promised to protect. "Damn him! If he has hurt her I swear I will not be responsible for my actions." His outburst caused a new wave of sobs from the distraught housekeeper.

"Oh sir! I'm sorry I couldn't save them, any of them. He hit me, see... and tied me up." There was much sniffing and gulping of air as Clementine attempted to relay the story amidst her crying. "I shouldn't have let him in. He said he was a doctor and you'd sent for him to attend to Miss Sally and Mr. Bromley before the nurse came tomorrow and..."

"Wait! He knew of Miss Carstairs appointment?"

Clementine gulped again.

"Yes sir, that's why I let him in. I thought he must be who he said he was. I feel such a fool! I heard her screaming for me... and I couldn't save her!" She broke down and he comforted her as best he could. Midnight knew she had been referring to Polly. The thought of the girl being so scared when he had promised to take care of her made him frantic. He *must* find her and Arthur and then he would...

There was a knock at the door.

"Sir? Your copy of Keats. Sorry to disturb you but I know it is urgent."

"Yes, thank you Giles. Could you accompany Mrs. Philips to the kitchen and make her some cocoa with brandy? I need some time to think."

"Of course, Sir. Come now Mrs. Phillips, let me help you." Giles came around the bed and held out his arm for her, she took it and rose shakily from the mattress.

"We must give them a proper burial sir, no paupers graves... please? They deserve better."

"They will have the best of funerals dear, kind Mrs. P. I promise you."

"There's something else, Sir."

Clementine held out her hand to him, something was curled inside her fist, she dropped it into his open palm. It was Polly's bracelet.

Midnight sat at his desk and poured over his copy of Keats' collection of poems. The Labrodite bracelet that had once belonged to his mother was in his pocket. He patted it and made a silent promise to Polly that he would find her and never let her out of his sight again.

Constable Rowe entered and informed him the resurrection men had arrived to remove the bodies.

"They will be kept at the mortuary until you can make the necessary funeral arrangements," he said.

"Thank you, constable. I'm much obliged."

"Any luck with the note?"

"A little. I need some information from you if you can?"

"What sort of information?"

"I need a list of names of men who were associated with

the British Medical Association, ones who have been discredited or struck off in the last five years or so. Is that possible?"

"I should think so. What is it for?"

Midnight related to Rowe the contents of the vision he had seen inside Mary's head,

"I believe your Spring-heeled Jack to be a doctor of some sort. Hemlock Nightingale is a ruse, an alias he uses to get close to his victims. This poem holds the key to finding the Inspector and Polly, I am sure of it. I feel like he *wants* me to find him, although I don't know why, yet. I need to know his real identity. It's a starting point at least until I can decipher the message within this poem."

"Consider it done. I'll go myself. We need to catch this bugger and hang him."

"Agreed."

"I'll go now, let you get on with that," Rowe pointed to the note on Gunn's desk. "The sooner I get that information, and you decipher that poem, the better. I'm sick of this bastard getting the better of us."

Midnight nodded and Constable Rowe retreated, leaving him alone with his thoughts. He read the poem a third time, hoping something might leap out at him. He listed what he already knew; *Hemlock Nightingale is an alias, he frequented the Rainbow Club, he used opium, he's harvesting souls, he's connected with the medical association, he's familiar with Keats...*

"What else... what else?" He muttered, tapping his pen on the desk.

He's an entertainer, a mesmerist, well spoken, a gentleman...

Something about that fact still irked him; what was an educated gentleman doing working as an entertainer? Even if he had been discredited or lost his profession, most gentlemen had money, land and family to live off. Why would a gentleman lower himself so, deliberately place himself among the common folk of Southwark?

The same reasons that I do?

But that didn't make any sense; Midnight shunned polite society in favour of the rowdy taverns, the filthy streets and the common folk because it gave him purpose. He found solace in the fact that he could build a hospital and dedicate his time and money to worthy causes. He knew how and where his money was best used because he placed himself amongst those in need. He aided Scotland Yard, tracked down murderers and solved crimes because it validated his uniqueness. He could be useful and do good things with both money and his powers.

"What are you up to Nightingale? What is your purpose?"

Midnight looked at the poem again, lines in the sixth and seventh stanza caught his eye,

'Now more than ever seems it rich to die,
To cease upon the midnight with no pain,
While thou art pouring forth thy soul abroad
In such ecstasy...
Thou wast not born for death, immortal Bird!'

An idea was forming in Midnight's mind, he read on and back again, looking for clues within the text.

'Here, where men sit and hear each other groan;
Where palsy shakes a few, sad, last grey hairs,
Where youth grows pale, and spectre-thin, and dies...
Away! Away! For I will fly to thee,
Not charioted by Bacchus and his pards,
But on the wings of Poesy...
And haply the Queen-Moon is on her throne,

Cluster'd around by all her starry Fays'

"Giles!" He jumped up from his desk and pulled hard and impatiently on the bell cord. "Giles? Hurry!" He paced the room until he heard nearing footsteps and then began chattering enthusiastically even as the butler entered the library. "Giles! Look, I think I have something," he scurried back to his desk and pointed to the poem. Giles stood next to him, his head bent to read it. "The first stanza is obvious; he talks of a higher state of consciousness, the use of hemlock as a poison like the story of Socrates." He glanced at Giles, who looked lost. "Socrates was put to death for corrupting the youth. He committed two acts that condemned him to death; he wouldn't acknowledge the Gods recognised by the city, and he introduced new deities. For this he was made to drink a brew of hemlock and died. In Nightingale's case, he swaps hemlock for opium. I believe the gods in the poem are Hemlocks' peers in the medical profession. And here in this line, *'One minute past, and Lethewards had sunk'*. Lethe is one of the five rivers in Hades. In Greek mythology if you drank from this river you lost your memories. Lethe was also the god of forgetfulness and oblivion. Are you seeing it yet?"

"Seeing what sir?" Giles shook his head.

"Lines nineteen to twenty, it speaks of wanting to drink the wine and fade away into the forest with the nightingale, to forget about all responsibility, society and work. The entire poem alludes to the nightingale being otherworldly; a spirit of the night, a symbol of beauty and immortality. Again, in Greek myth, Philomel the king's daughter was mutilated before the Gods turned her into a nightingale to set her free. In Keats poem, he laments the nightingale's freedom and envies the immortality of its song. Do you see now Giles? This is why

Hemlock Nightingale is harvesting souls, he thinks he can become immortal!"

"Is such a thing possible?"

"It shouldn't be. But then neither should I be," he replied in a serious tone.

"I can see your point sir. So, why has he taken Miss Polly and Inspector Gredge? Does he intend to have their souls too?"

"Polly is his Philomel, *'Thou wast not born for death immortal Bird!'* I've no doubt he sees her amputation as representative of the loss of Philomel's tongue. When he harvests his victims' souls he leaves them mute, devoid of personalities. They are mere hollows of their former selves. Their souls are his gateway to immortality. How? I don't know yet. As for Arthur, I don't believe he has any other use for him than as a bargaining chip."

"And what is he bargaining for exactly?"

"Me I think... although I'm not sure why."

"What else can you glean from the poem?"

Midnight's attention went back to the text.

"Here:

'Where palsy shakes a few, sad, last grey hairs, where youth grows pale, and spectre-thin, and dies.'
He's not just referring to the bleakness of the physical world around him, the poverty, disease and death, Keats often speaks of time as his enemy in his poetry and this is what these lines refer to – the cruelty of time."

"Mm-hmm, I see that. Immortality once again?"

"Exactly, Giles! This line here is interesting too, look:

'Not charioted by Bacchus and his pards, but on the view-less wings of Poesy'

Bacchus is Dionysus; god of the grape harvest, wine, madness and *theatre!* Keats is saying that he will not ride on Bacchus chariot to the afterlife but will reach it by his own means – his 'Poesy' or poetry. I think this is what Hemlock is trying to do; construct some means of using harvested souls in exchange for immortality. Ever heard of the cult of Dionysus? They worshipped the God in ancient Greece and Rome. They would partake in ritual, theatrical dances and music. The aim of it was to free the souls and minds of people marginalized or shunned by society; they were also referred to as '*The Cult of Souls'.*"

Giles took a moment and then asked, "But is it the souls of his victims or his own he wishes to free?"

"Perhaps both? Who knows. But it's starting to make sense now. Ode to a Nightingale is all about how Keats laments the immortality and beauty of the nightingale and his song; how its song transcends the realms of everyday life and reaches far beyond. I'm convinced Hemlock sees himself as a martyred victim. If Rowe can give me names of doctors who have been discredited, I'm betting we can find our Hemlock, or whatever his real name is, on that list!"

"But aside from trying to make himself immortal, what is his motive? Why would a mesmerist, discredited doctor or not, want to become immortal?"

"This is something we need to uncover, Giles, and we need that list of names to begin."

19

DISCOVERIES

Midnight hated waiting. He hated feeling helpless. Rowe had still not called with any news from the British Medical Association and it had been nearly eighteen hours since last night's murders and Polly's kidnap. He hadn't slept. Mrs. Phillips had been put to bed and he'd given Giles instructions to tell her to stay put and rest. Giles had seen to breakfast – tea and scones, not the usual feast but it was most welcome all the same. The butler had kept him company until just after one o'clock and then retired, leaving Midnight alone. He had dozed off in the parlour's fireside armchair sometime after four but was awake again an hour later, and he spent the next few hours either pacing the room or poring over the poem. He could find nothing new amongst the lines of text, no clue as to where Hemlock might be holding his captives or what personal message he may be trying to send Midnight. By lunchtime Mrs. Phillips had risen and was insisting on continuing with her duties, despite Midnight's protestations she declared that no invader would prevent her from going about her daily business and so she trotted off with a determined step to the kitchen to prepare a late lunch. Soon after, Giles had brought the afternoon post, which at least contained *some* good news, although Midnight felt it little consolation considering the more immediately pressing matter of finding Arthur and Polly.

"Construction of our hospital is to begin next week." Midnight's flat tone emphasised his lack of enthusiasm.

"That is a good thing sir."

"I suppose so." He sighed.

"You'll be helping many of London's poor and needy, of course it's a good thing. You should be proud."

"How far have we got with sourcing potential staff and doctors?"

"I have informed the board of directors at St. Thomas' that we will be needing nurses potentially within the next twelve to eighteen months. The Nightingales complete a year of training at the new nursing school there and then they are usually allocated positions post-graduation. I felt it best to..."

"Stop!" Midnight shouted and sprang from his chair, eyes wide.

"Sir?"

"Repeat what you just said, about the nurses."

"That I have informed..." Giles began

"No! What you called them, the graduates?"

"The Nightingales... oh!" Now it was Giles' turn to stare open-mouthed.

"Exactly!" Midnight slurped down the rest of his cup of tea and set the cup down with a satisfied grin. "Send a runner to Constable Rowe, I think we may have just discovered a lead!"

The doorbell rang. Giles looked at Midnight.

"Perhaps that's Rowe after all! Good, now we can get on with things without waiting any longer! Go and let him in please Giles?" He waited eagerly for the appearance of the constable so he could tell him what he'd uncovered but it was not Rowe that came back through the door with Giles, it was a woman. Midnight stared blankly at her. Giles coughed and introduced her.

"Miss Carstairs, your Lordship." He announced with raised eyebrows.

"Carstairs... Carstairs?" Why did that name ring a bell?

"The nurse, sir."

"Oh, dear God! Of course. I am so sorry Miss Carstairs, please forgive me, I have rather a lot on my mind of late. Do sit down." He flustered a little as he pulled out a chair; he had completely forgotten she was due to arrive this morning.

"Pleased to meet you, your Lordship." She had a pleasant, calming tone to her voice and a no-nonsense, polite smile.

"Um..." said Midnight, not sure where to start. "I am afraid you have had a wasted journey madam." She gave him a questioning look. "You see the patients we hired you to care for are no longer with us."

"Oh," she said simply, "I see."

"They passed away yesterday you see and... well, I'm afraid I forgot to send word to your erm... your..." he turned to Giles. "Where is it exactly that we hired Miss Carstairs from?" he felt slightly abashed that he didn't know – he'd left the hiring to Giles and Mrs. Philips. Giles held a very odd expression, as if he had suddenly realised something.

"St Thomas' hospital Sir, from the new nursing college of Miss Florence Nightingale." The silent look that passed between himself and Giles was loaded with understanding, Midnight addressed Miss Carstairs once more.

"Dear lady, might I ask you how long how you been in training at the nursing school? It may seem a little impertinent, but I assure you it is of the utmost importance."

"Well, I was a nurse at St Thomas' for two years before Miss Nightingale opened her school this past July, I enrolled as soon as it opened. Miss Nightingale is a pioneer in her field, her methods and theories on hygiene have transformed the nursing profession. We girls never got proper training before. All we did was mop floors, change bedpans, bedding and bandages. However, I was allowed to assist the doctors on their rounds," she said proudly. "I was given special dispensation to take this position on account of my experience. Matron said I could train on the job."

"Indeed, I hear great things about Miss Nightingale and her work in the Crimea. So, you have worked at St. Thomas' for a little over two years?"

"Yes Sir."

"And in that time, did you know of any doctors who were involved in any scandal or were struck off the register?" Miss Carstairs looked shocked at the impropriety of his question so he did his best to reassure her. "I understand the question is somewhat odd, please be assured it is relevant to the passing of two of the patients you were hired to care for. I fear they may have fallen victim to one such doctor and you may have vital information that could help us. Can you think of anyone?"

She sat in thought for a minute or two before she made her hesitant reply.

"Why, in truth, I can think of only one and his termination of employment was not particularly scandalous, more a quiet push out the door if you will."

"His name?" he breathed,

"Doctor Giling. I worked on his ward for a time. It wasn't open very long though on account of... well, I don't rightly know in truth, but I heard the governors weren't happy with some of his practices. But that was only hearsay."

"Which ward Miss Carstairs? What branch of medicine did he practice?"

"At first it was general surgery sir, but then Doctor Giling became interested in maladies of the mind."

"Psychiatry?"

"Yes sir."

"Interesting. Has he ever work at the city asylums?"

"I'm sorry, I don't know."

"Are you still in touch with Doctor Giling?"

"I was. Not any more though. I used to volunteer down at the mission house in Southwark. Doctor Giling volunteered there too. Well, he's not really a doctor now but he offered his services free to the mission, you see. It wasn't like they could afford to pay a proper doctor."

"And you told him about your appointment here, at this house?"

Miss Carstairs blanched, the notion had struck her that something was amiss and it may involve her and Doctor Giling.

"Ye... yes Sir," she stammered, now unsure of what the implications of her answers might be, "I told him I wasn't able to help out at the mission any more, and I thought he'd be angry on account of the other girl leaving so suddenly."

"There was another?"

She nodded, reluctant now to divulge what she knew. The atmosphere in the room had begun to change, the air felt stifling, the light a little dimmer. She fiddled nervously with her purse strings

"Miss Carstairs, I insist you tell me."

"She was a well-to-do lady, Doctor Giling brought her along to help her, to give her a sense of purpose he said, but she didn't stay long. She stopped coming after a while, we never saw her again."

"Emeline Rowbotham!" Midnight and Giles said at the same time.

"You know her? What happened to her, where did she go?"

"I'm sorry to say she died, madam." Midnight spared her the truth; it served no purpose to frighten the woman. Then again, he did not want her going back to the mission and meeting Hemlock. "Miss Carstairs, I told you that two of the patients here had passed away, however, I have a housekeeper who suffered a very great fright and a nasty bump on the head yesterday. I'd feel so much better if you were able to stay here for a few days at least and keep an eye on her? There is a missing child too, Polly, that I hope to recover very soon. She may also need a nurse upon her return. Would this arrangement be agreeable to you?"

"I confess it would sir. I had given notice at my quarters at the school, they had agreed to let me finish my training in-house here but they might allow me my old room back."

"I am sorry. Please do stay here as long as we need you? If the time comes when..." *when what? You don't get Polly back?* He shook his head. No, he could not allow himself such thoughts. "Please stay?" He said simply. To his relief, she agreed. "Giles will show you to your room and introduce you to our housekeeper, Mrs. Philips."

Giles raised an eyebrow. Midnight could tell by his expression that he wasn't sure what kind of reception Nurse Carstairs would get from Clementine Philips, especially if she ordered her back to bed.

"Much obliged sir"

"This way madam." Giles took nurse Carstairs' bags and led her out of the room while Midnight jotted down a note for Constable Rowe. Giles would task a runner with delivering the note and he hoped it wouldn't take too long for Rowe to arrive. He needed more information about this Doctor Giling before he could start looking for Polly and Gredge.

As late afternoon turned to early evening, Midnight grew

more and more agitated. When the great hall clock struck six Rowe finally arrived, flustered and apologetic.

"I am sorry for not returning sooner Mr. Gunn. It's been a nightmare down at the station. The Commissioner's in uproar about the murder of your two house guests and the discovery of Mary's body. We've all had a right old dressing down about our inability to capture this bastard. The paperwork has been unbelievable."

"Did you discover anything?" Midnight's tone was clipped, he struggled to rein in his impatience even though he felt a pang of guilt for Rowe. He was connected with all three of those deaths in one way or another and he felt guilty for any recriminations that may fall upon Rowe. Locating Polly and Gredge was paramount, however, and he had no time to waste on small talk.

"I have your list right here." Rowe presented him with a single sheet of paper, containing only three names and a brief explanation of the terms of their termination of employment. Midnight saw Giling's name at the top.

"Doctor Ethan Giling, this is him."

"How do you know?" asked Rowe.

"Long story. I discovered his surname but now we have his Christian name, residential address and field of work. Excellent!"

"Mmm, the street address didn't pan out I'm afraid. It's an old boarding house, closed six months ago and he left no forwarding address. What about the poem?"

"Damn! That is a shame. I'll get to the poem in a minute... See here," Midnight jotted down the letters of Ethan Giling's name and began to rearrange them, he turned the paper around so Rowe could see, "Nightingale! It's an anagram."

"Like that poem you have?"

"Like the poem, and many other things. Let me show you what I discovered."

Midnight showed Rowe how he had interpreted Keats' poem and how everything pointed to the notorious Spring-Heeled Jack as a seeker of immortality and harvester of souls. And how nurse Carstairs had helped connect him to St Thomas' hospital and a mission in Southwark.

"Spring-Heeled Jack, Hemlock Nightingale and Ethan Giling? Blimey how many names does one man need? So, you reckon he met Miss Rowbotham at the Rainbow club, talked her into volunteering at the mission and then killed her?"

"It makes sense to me. I think up until then he had been content merely harvesting souls and leaving them hollow but alive. I believe Miss Rowbotham's death was accidental, perhaps he squeezed a little too hard for too long. But now he's killed Mary, Sally and Billy I think he has a taste for it. Was he attempting to cover his tracks with their murders? Or perhaps Sally and Billy were meant as provocation? Who knows. One thing I can't work out is if Ethan Giling is human, how has he been sucking the souls out of people and what is he doing with the souls once he's harvested them?"

"I might have an idea," said Rowe. "The commissioner had us go back to the Old Vic and search it since the given street address for Doctor Giling isn't viable. We found some very strange contraptions locked in those dressing rooms; things I can't explain. Perhaps you'd like to come and have a look?"

"I's a starting point, it may give us some idea of where he is now and what he intends to do. I have a feeling Giling lost his profession because he was dabbling in something *unorthodox*, those contraptions you speak of may give us some clue. I have heard of mesmerists using strange machines and gadgetry in their shows to prove the existence of an afterlife. I suspect

Giling was involved in something like that and has perhaps found a way to prove it!"

"Blimey! That would be a turn up. Are you bringing the butler again?" Rowe asked. His dry tone was lost on Midnight, who was used to the company and assistance of Giles when required.

"No, I'll need him to remain and watch over my house-keeper and the nurse, I'll not leave poor Mrs. Philips alone again."

"Very well, we'll leave now then. Where to first? Theatre or the mission? Only I've no lads with me, so it'll *just* be us."

Midnight caught the deliberate inflection in Rowe's voice this time.

"Is that a problem?"

"No, it's just... you know," Rowe shrugged. "I've got eyes. I've seen things around you, I know you ain't, you know... like me."

"How observant Constable Rowe," came a steely reply. "I ask again, is that a problem?"

"Bugger, no! That's what I'm saying. Finding the Inspector and the girl is more important than anything. So, if it's just us, you can do whatever you must this evening and I'm none the wiser, if you catch my drift."

20

TIME AND TIDE

The sound of lapping water roused her. It wasn't a gentle noise but harsh and urgent and every now and then the lapping was interrupted by a laborious sucking sound. The second thing she noticed was how cold she felt. The icy October wind battered her body and caused her hair to flail madly. It was dark aside from a few twinkling lights in the distance. She tried to move but ropes bit into her flesh. She threw her head back to scream and her skull connected with hard stone. Panic filled her.

Where am I?

"Mista' Midnight! Help me!" Polly struggled against her bonds, her hair whipped at her frozen face, she couldn't see, she couldn't feel her feet... where were her feet? "Please? Someone?"

"Who's there?"

A man's voice came from out of the dark, carried on the howling wind, she barely heard it.

"Mista' Midnight? It's me, Polly!"

An eerie disembodied groan followed causing her heart to quicken. She tried to peer into the darkness to ascertain where the voice was coming from, but a heavy fog had settled around her.

"Polly? The girl staying with Mr. Gunn?"

"Ye... yes," she stammered, "Who's that? Can you help me?"

"Polly, my name is Inspector Gredge. I'm a friend of Mr. Gunn. Are you alright? Where are you? I can't see you."

"Can you get me out please 'Spector? I'm really cold."

"I'm afraid I can't, I'm tied to something but I'm here with you. Don't be afraid. Help will be along soon."

"I've lost me feet! I can't feel 'em. I think I'm dying 'Spector."

"It's the cold child, you'll be alright do you hear? Just keep talking to me."

"I want to go 'ome." Polly sobbed. The chill in her bones had soaked through to her core and she began to feel drowsy. Despite the battering wind she felt her eyes grow heavy and her head lolled forward onto her chest. After a few moments, she came to.

"Polly! Polly! Do you hear me? Come on child, listen to my voice and stay awake!" There was no sound other than the unrelenting gurgle of the water and Gredge's chattering teeth. "Polly!"

"Yes 'Spector?"

"Mr. Gunn. Was he at home, is he alright?" Gredge had not seen Midnight since that night at the Rainbow. He had no idea if his friend was even alive.

"Well, he was but then he left with Mista' Morgan."

Thank God

"He'll be here soon," he lied. "Why don't you tell me how you like Meriton House? How is your Mr. Midnight?" Racking sobs came back to him, "What is it Polly, do you not like it at there?"

"I like it true 'nuff 'Spector, it's just that he found me. And

Mista' Midnight promised he wouldn't and then he... he killed them others and I thought he was gonna kill me too! And now we're both stuck 'ere! Are we gonna die 'Spector?"

"No Polly, I won't let that happen and neither with Mr. Gunn. Just keep talking to me and try not to fall asleep alright?"

"Alright, I'll try," came her small voice in reply

"Polly, what did you mean about someone killing the others? What others? Has something happened at the house?"

"The devil man came, the one who got me before. He knobbled old Missus Phillips and then I heard him get Miss Sally and Mista Billy. I tried to hide in the cupboard but he found me. He made me look at him and everythin' went dark and then I woke up 'ere."

Gredge realised he had missed a lot. God only knew what had been going on in his absence. He tried to reconcile the fact that if Midnight had escaped the clutches of Chinese Mary and the Rainbow and had made it home, he would stop at nothing until he found Polly. The fact that someone had gotten into his house and committed murder would drive his friend to the brink of combustion. What he couldn't work out was how he and Polly had both ended up here in the water. There must be some connection between the killer and Mary.

"Polly? Do you know what this devil-man looks like?"

"Sort of... he's got a swirly moustache and a pointy beard. His face was covered mostly, but his eyes were bright red... 'cept at the 'sylum. Then he was just covered in grease paint so I couldn't properly tell."

"The performer?"

"Yes." A blast of freezing wind hit them and Polly shivered so violently she thought her teeth would fall out. "I'm so cold 'Spector," she chattered.

"I know child, so am I. Don't worry, try to focus on my voice. Can you see me?"

"Not quite, it's too foggy. Where are we?"

"I think we're in the river."

"The river? I can't swim 'Spector!" She struggled against her bonds again, the rope grazing her flesh, although this time she couldn't feel it.

Unless we get free of this rope it won't matter if either of us can swim, Gredge thought. A wave of water hit his shin, it had been below his ankles not so long ago.

"Polly, can you feel the water on you?"

"It's up to me knees!"

Shit! The tide's coming in. For God's sake Midnight, wherever you are, bloody hurry up!

Gredge tried shouting for help but the wind and fog swallowed it.

Keep the child talking, if she goes silent the cold might take her, unless the tide takes her first.

"Help is coming, don't worry. Tell me about the man at the asylum?"

"He was doing tricks and that, making 'em all laugh. But I knew he was there for me. He came to find me."

"Did Mr. Gunn say anything to you about him? Or did you see any other policemen at the house?"

"Can't 'member seeing anyone else but Mista' Midnight did mention a constable. He was off to meet him or something, down The Old Vic... Least, that what he said to Missus Philips. I don't reckon I was meant to hear that, but I was listening see, on account of I'd seen that devil's mush on the poster Mista' Midnight had. I wanted to make sure he was going to make him go away like he promised...only he didn't." She sounded so forlorn. "I'm tired 'Spector."

"Now listen! I have known your Mr. Midnight for a while

now young lady and you must understand, if he made you a promise he will keep it. If what you say is true, then he will be looking for that bad man already and that means he won't be long in finding you. Don't you lose faith now, you must trust me. He *will* come."

God, please let him come!

There was no reply from the girl, only the lonely lapping of the water that crept higher as the minutes passed. Gredge's mind raced, it must be Rowe that Polly had overheard Midnight mention. That meant they were onto a lead. Rowe was a good lad, smart too. If Midnight and Rowe were investigating something and Polly had identified the killer, surely their rescue was imminent? Something niggled him, he couldn't answer the question as to why this villain had tied them up and left them to the river. Even if Gunn and Rowe apprehended the sick bastard, what would he gain from leaving them both here? Why hadn't he killed them already?

No Arthur, you need to ask yourself why the fuck are we still alive.

21

THE HUNT

I n the bowels of The Old Vic, a fusty dressing room at the end of a dark corridor held a treasure so horrifying that the two men who discovered it could not believe their eyes. Gunn and Rowe had arrived at The Old Vic to find it still in its empty state and under police cordon; the discovery of Mary's body and the things in Hemlock's dressing room had forced them to close it off while the investigation was ongoing.

The dressing rooms had been locked when Midnight had investigated the theatre with Giles and he hadn't had chance to look inside once they had found Mary because Rowe had arrived bearing the terrible news of kidnap and murder. The room in which they now stood looked like any other theatre dressing room, aside from the two large armchairs on the right side of the room and a few bookshelves containing such titles as 'Mesmerism As A Cure' and 'Cleansing The Maladies Of The Mind'. One book in particular Midnight found very interesting,

"The Testament of Solomon?" Rowe asked.

"Hmm, do you know the story of King Solomon, Constable?"

"Can't say that I do. What is it about?"

"A demon. The king discovered a demon was taking pay, food, and the life force of a young boy so he prayed to God and God gave him a ring with a magical seal on it. It allowed Solomon to capture the demon and have him do his bidding."

"That's in the Bible?" Rowe sounded incredulous.

"No, it is not. There are possible allusions to it in Matthew but Solomon's testament remains as you see it here; it stands alone. Often connected with the occult because of its demonic associations."

"And you think this is significant because?"

"Because I've been wondering how Nightingale has been harvesting souls and this may be a clue."

"You think he has some sort of demonic power?"

"Not he himself, he is human, of that I'm sure, but perhaps he has found a way to use a dark power to extract souls. It's not beyond the realms of possibility. You can trust me on that."

Rowe looked very uncomfortable. Midnight supposed Rowe could just about accept his *eccentricities* because he was on their side. He had to admit; the prospect of Hemlock holding such power did not sit well.

There were leaflets for the Southwark mission house where Hemlock volunteered; a place where the poor and destitute could find shelter, treatment, food and God. It was highly likely that is where Hemlock found some of his victims. Maps, and diagrams of fantastical contraptions and gadgetry lay strewn around the room, including a camera. He found a group of photographs that were pinned to the wall. They were of people undergoing surgical procedures. Nightingale was in the pictures, alone. Upon closer inspection, he could see a faint mist surrounding each of the patients. The last photograph made his skin prickle – the mist had a face! Midnight picked up one of the diagrams, it showed a piece of machinery, cylindrical in shape with glass canisters held in place around its exterior, various pipes were attached to the top to what appeared to be a small crystal-powered generator. He'd never seen anything like it before.

"What is it?" Rowe asked.

"A storage container."

"For what?"

He didn't reply but pointed to the inked label on the paper. Rowe squinted at the tiny inked letters and gasped.

"Souls!"

"Yes. The question is, Constable, where is it? It must be in use – we know Hemlock has harvested souls already but where is he keeping them?"

"Can't be anywhere here, me and the lads searched every nook and cranny."

"Let's have another look around."

The gas lighting was on this time, the Yard had made sure the lights were accessible since they'd cordoned off the building. It made things a lot easier for them to make their way around. They started in the cellar where Gredge had been held and Mary's body found. It seemed like the obvious place, but their search turned up nothing. Next, they examined each of the four dressing rooms to no avail, only Hemlock's showed any signs of recent occupation.

"There are two manager's offices upstairs, they're on the top floor overlooking the circle. We could try there?" Rowe showed Gunn to the once grand staircase that led to the circle and the upper floors. A semi-circular corridor encompassed the rear of the top floor seating area that overlooked the stage, the heavy, moth-eaten red velvet stage curtains were open and the stage had been prepped for the next performance.

"This way Mr. Gunn. The offices are just to the left through this arch."

Midnight opened the door marked 'Manager' hopeful that one of these room would offer up a clue to the whereabouts of either Arthur and Polly, Hemlock's plans or the storage device.

"There is nothing here either. Damn!" Midnight slammed his fist on an old desk sending up a cloud of dust. "There has to be something somewhere! He left that poem for me, he *wants* me to find him, and I know it!"

"We've looked everywhere Mr. Gunn. Perhaps we need to concentrate our search elsewhere, St Thomas' perhaps?"

"This is his stage Rowe, his domain. He's laid out his props for his audience. He's just waiting for the rest of the cast members to turn up for the grand finale. I just wish I knew what my lines were."

"We could check his dressing room again, perhaps we missed something?"

"It's worth a look I suppose," Midnight replied, disheartened at the lack of evidence, bar a few maps and diagrams, that the theatre had turned up. He walked back with Rowe through the arch into the corridor that encircled the upper circle. Glimpsing the top of the red stage curtain over the top of the balcony, he stopped.

"Mr. Gunn? What is it?" Rowe watched as Gunn walked steadily towards the balcony and rested his hands on the carved wooden railing. There he stood, his back towards the constable, for at least half a minute before he spoke.

"The *stage*. Constable Rowe, come here and tell me what you see."

Rowe stood next to Gunn and gazed down upon the large stage. It had been set with the props ready for Hemlock's next opening act.

"I must be missing something. What is it you've seen?"

"This is his stage."

"Yes?"

"Look at it... the boards, see anything?"

Midnight grew impatient as Rowe peered down at the wooden boards from their lofty position.

"Bloody 'ell! It never occurred to me to look..."

"Nor I. Let's not beat ourselves up about it now. Let's get down there and see what lies beneath!"

As they descended the two flights of stairs Midnight grew more and more confident that something important was hidden underneath that stage, he could sense it. He cursed himself for allowing desperation and panic to rule his actions rather than using his senses. But then again, he'd never been this personally involved in a case before. There was a child to consider – *his* child, as Polly now legally was – and it was distracting. He needed to think with a clear head, her life was at stake and possibly Arthur's too.

Within two feet of the stage area he felt it; a pulsing energy washed over him like a gentle wave, teasing, calling him forward. The shadows on the walls twitched but he blocked them out, this energy felt pure. Drawing in a few threads of light from the gas lamps he reached out to the energy source. The moment the two fields collided the mood changed; the latent pulsing became a barrage of anxiety and despair so powerful it almost overwhelmed him. Midnight climbed onto the boards and got to his knees to pull open the trapdoor.

"Careful Sir," Rowe whispered, as if he could also sense the change in atmosphere. "He might be down there, hiding. Perhaps I should go first?"

Midnight shook his head,

"No, it's not him... it's something else. I feel it." He ran his hand over the trapdoor trying to feel if the energy was benevolent. It was hard to tell for certain. It seemed, in his mind's eye, to be in turmoil. He had a mental image of a broiling whirlpool of emotions so strong now he felt compelled to go to it. It was impossible to resist even if he'd wanted to. Rowe held open the door as Midnight climbed inside the black hole beneath the stage. Drawing in more threads of light he made a small fireball to illuminate his surroundings. It was squat under there; the space, although it stretched the full length of the boards, seemed pokey to him and he had to bend his head to traverse the narrow walkway. There was a thud behind him as Rowe jumped in after him.

"See anything?"

"Nothing yet. It's this way." Striding ahead into the gloom, the small fireball floated ahead to light the way. He had taken a mere ten steps when a glint of something golden caught his eye. "Here!" They both hurried forwards as the scene unfolded before them with sickening clarity. In this crypt-like underbelly of The Old Vic stood a device comparable to that of the diagram they had found in the dressing room. The glint had come from the large brass cylinder that held several glass containers full of a slightly opaque-looking, blue-white substance which swirled frantically at their approach.

"Good God... are they?" Rowe gulped unable to finish his question.

"The souls of Spring-Heeled Jack's victims?" Midnight finished it for him. "I believe they are Constable." As he stared into the writhing mass of bright mist, individual voices became apparent to him. These were not voices that could be heard; they were inside of him. As one soul after another called out to him, pleading for either release or to be united with the physical body it belonged to, he found he could not hold back his tears. He felt such sorrow and shame that one human being could inflict such torment on another. He opened himself to their energies and felt the essence of each individual touch him, their identities became clear; Sally-Anne Smithers, Billy Bromley, Laura Carter, Charlie Fenwick,

Milly O'Neil. Alice Jane Fairbanks and Emeline Rowbotham. Of those seven victims only two remained alive as far he knew. He hoped beyond hope that after tonight, he would find a way to return their souls to them. He hadn't saved Sal or Billy when they'd been in his care or any of the others for that matter... but he had saved Polly,

"We must save them Rowe. The ones who are left and Polly and Arthur. We must save them all."

22

THE MISSION

"Rowe, you must go! We cannot leave these souls to his mercy. What if he should return? I will go to the mission alone. You get a message to M division to send more officers to guard the theatre. You can meet me at the mission house thereafter."

"What if something should go wrong? Or you're not at the mission when I come looking?"

"In that case, you look for my note; I will leave a message there telling you where I have gone."

Rowe considered this, his hand travelled back and forth across his chin and he shook his head.

"I don't like it. We should stick together. Too many things could go wrong."

"I don't like it either but we don't have time to wait for reinforcements. Time is of the essence. I will go on alone until you can meet me. I'm not willing to negotiate on this constable. The mission is the next place I must go, it's a short walk from here and closer than St Thomas'. The victims, aside from Rowbotham, were all poor as church mice, and where better to find church mice than at a mission?"

Rowe relented, "Very well but you leave a note so I can follow you, is that clear?"

"Crystal."

They parted ways on the steps of The Old Vic; Rowe running as fast as he could to notify his comrades at M division, as Midnight turned right and headed in the direction of the Southwark Mission House. The fog was rolling in. Soon it would be too thick to see properly, and it was bitterly cold. He walked at a rapid pace to keep out the October chill. Something wet touched his cheek and seconds later it happened again. Looking skywards he saw it had begun to snow. He couldn't put a finger on why, but suddenly he knew his task had become altogether more urgent. He broke into a run and it took him only five minutes to reach his destination.

A soft glow emitted from the windows of the mission house, it would be occupied on this night as always by Southwark's destitute, who had constant need of the shelter and support it offered. Situated next to the church of St Andrews, potatoes baked in their skins were on offer from breakfast throughout the day until late in the evening. As well as small cups of tea, coffee for the adults and milk for the children who also received bowls of steaming stew as an evening meal. If you had a few pennies you could buy a bed for the night and a breakfast of eggs, sausages and a warm roll. Prayers were at sunrise, noon and dusk and were compulsory, as were the Sunday school teachings for youngsters. The mission was the last ray of hope for some, the final defence between living or dying. The nuns of St. Andrews rarely turned anyone away. If you hadn't enough pennies for a bed you were offered the floor and the leaning rope for halfpence where, arms hanging over it and arse on the hard stone, you could attempt sleep. Midnight had never visited this mission, but most were renowned for being unsanitary, flea-ridden cesspits. The nuns and volunteers tried their best to provide shelter, hot food, and somewhere to wash, but there were no toilets. If you were lucky enough to have a bed you had your own pot to piss in, but the half-penny sit-ups had a bucket in the corner which everyone shared. In mid-October, even the stench of shit and a rope to rest on was preferable to spending the night on the frozen streets.

It must have been nearing 9pm, which meant they would be locking their doors in an hour. He rapped on the front entrance and waited until one of the Sisters opened the peep-hole and asked who it was. When she saw a well-to-do gentleman outside she didn't hesitate to open the door for him.

"Good evening to you Sir, what is it I can do for you?"

"Good evening Sister. My name is Mr. Gunn of Meriton house, Berkeley Square. Might I come in and have a word?"

The sister stepped aside and let him inside the small entrance hall. She showed him to a small study, her office most likely, and bade him sit down.

"I confess it is not unheard of for a lady or a gentleman such as yourself to offer assistance to us but I'm not usually accustomed to it being at such a late hour. We have already served supper and are bedding down for the evening. I'm afraid there's not much you can do. Perhaps you would prefer to return in the morning?"

"Apologies Sister. It is not aid I come to offer tonight. It is your assistance I require. A good friend of mine, a police Inspector, is missing and I need your help." He had used Gredge as bait hoping that she would be more inclined to offer information on Hemlock if the police were involved.

"Police? We're never short of them around this area Mr. Gunn. How is it you think I can help?"

"You once had a doctor here, volunteering his expertise I believe? A Doctor Ethan Giling?"

"Doctor Giling? Why yes, what is it you want with him?"

"I... have a few questions I'd like to put to him. Would you perhaps know where I might find him? I have a listed street address, but it is old and not in the area."

"Why, he is here Mr. Gunn. Would you like me to fetch him?"

Midnight, stunned beyond belief at Hemlock's brazen display of confidence, merely nodded. When the good Sister had shut the door, he flew to his feet enraged! The shadows leaped, ready to be called upon. He could not believe that murdering bastard would leave himself so exposed to capture like this. He'd wrongly assumed that Hemlock would be in hiding by now. If only he and Rowe had come here first! He would snap him in half for what he had done, he would torture him slowly until he begged for mercy, until he screamed for forgiveness. He would...

"Good evening Mr. Gunn," came the cool, calm voice of a killer. Midnight swung around to face the door, took one step towards Hemlock and prepared to throw everything he had at him. Hemlock held up a hand. "You'll never find them if you kill me."

The statement caused Midnight's step to falter. He clenched his fists tightly trying to get control over the shadows.

"Where are they?" he demanded.

"I will tell you if you come with me."

"If you have hurt either of them I swear I will rip you apart!"

"Then we had better hurry Mr. Gunn. Follow me if you please."

Hemlock left the room and Midnight stormed after him;

forgetting all about Rowe's promised note. They exited the mission and headed across the green to St. Andrews. The snow was falling in gentle flurries now and the church was in darkness. They didn't go through the main entrance but through a small door to the side of the building. They walked in silence, the atmosphere charged with one-sided anger. Midnight could sense excitement emanating from Hemlock, which made him even more furious.

"Well? Where are they?" he spat, as Hemlock led him past the pews and to an area behind the alter.

"Not far now, down here." He was pointing to a large hole in the floor from which he could see stone steps descending into the dark.

"After you." If this bastard thought he would step blindly into an underground space with an enemy at his back then he was a fool. Hemlock grinned knowingly and inclined his head in mock bow. As he disappeared into the blackness, Midnight thought how easy it would be to give him a little push.

The shadows pulsed as if they were anticipating a fight. He held them off as best he could but his emotions battled with him to accept them. Deep down he wanted nothing more than to unleash merry hell upon the man who had kidnapped his friend, committed murder and taken his Polly. *Wait, just until they are safe and then you can have him,* he told himself, *then you can kill him!*

Hemlock stopped at the foot of the stairs and struck a match. He lit a candle in the wall sconce, walked a few feet further and lit another and another until their surroundings were swathed in a warm, flickering glow. Hemlock was now on the opposite side to him; the space was circular and stone plinths stood around the room. The walls had large rectangular holes built into them big enough for coffins, although there were none now. They were in the crypt beneath St. Andrews. Midnight looked around but saw no sign of either Polly or Arthur.

"I shall ask you one last time *Doctor Giling,* where are they?"

Instead of answering, Hemlock gave him a sideways smile and retrieved an iron box with intricate silver carvings on it from one of the recesses. He held it out to Midnight.

"Your answer lies in here Mr. Gunn. Come, look."

Midnight strode forward, sick of this game and sick of wasting time. He reached the middle of the room and suddenly felt his body slam into an invisible wall. It knocked him backwards. Had he hit glass? He stepped forward again with the same result. He tried to go sideways and then in reverse but he could not move in any direction, he was trapped! Laughter reached him and he looked up to see Hemlock clap his hands together in mock applause.

"Well, I must say Mr. Gunn, I find myself quite disappointed that you made it so easy! Perhaps I have over-estimated you?"

"What have you done?" Midnight's fury was raging inside of him. He could see the shadows dancing and he called on them. He would blast this brigand into a thousand pieces. He readied himself for the familiar pain of acceptance, but it didn't come. He tried again – and nothing happened. He looked at the shadows and realised with horror that the shadows were not dancing for him, it was merely the flickering of candlelight on the walls of the crypt. "No!" he shouted and flung himself at the invisible barrier. "What is this?" Hemlock did not answer, he looked up towards the ceiling. Midnight followed his gaze and saw a pentagram painted in red, directly overhead, the circumference of which was adorned with various runic symbols and glyphs. He knew enough of the occult to know this was a demon trap of some kind. He was confused; he was not a demon so why would it work on him? But it must be the trap that was blocking him from using his powers.

"I have one at last!" Hemlock shouted gleefully, "I can finally make my bargain."

"One what? What bargain?"

"Oh, come now, let's not pretend anymore. You have something I want and I have payment for it. Why don't we curtail the niceties and get on with the transaction, hmm?"

"Something you want?"

"Immortality, Mr. Gunn! And you, you demon spawn will give it to me or I will allow your little pet and the policeman to die."

Polly! The candlelight flared briefly but only Midnight noticed. He discretely opened himself to the light and he immediately felt its tender touch. It was only his dark power that this trap affected, he still had the light! Would it work though? His dark powers had always dominated and he used his light only to soothe and heal. Still, it was better than nothing. Now he had to play Hemlock's game. He must discover where Polly and Arthur were hidden and then he would break free.

"I cannot give you immortality. I am not a god."

"I know what you are, demon! I have a gift you will not be able to resist. I have the spells to command you and if you don't do as I ask your little injured bird will die."

"First you must tell me why?"

"Why?"

"Why you want to be immortal. Why you murdered those innocent people and why you think I can help you. I want to know it all, from the moment you first had the idea to harvest souls, why you murdered Emeline and Mary, killed Sally and Billy in my house, why you haven't murdered the child and how you discovered what I am. You tell me everything, including where the girl and the Inspector are, and I will help you."

Hemlock's eyes lit up.

"I knew it! I knew you were one of them. I saw what happened at the asylum. You made the shadows move. I felt your power and from that moment on I knew you had to be to be the one. It was the sign I had prayed for."

"Our Dark Lord answers his faithful servants. Now, keep talking." He needed Hemlock to be distracted so he could draw in more of the light and be ready to break out the instant he learned where Polly and Gredge were. "Why were you removed from your position at St. Thomas'?"

"Pah! They did not appreciate my talents. I was a great surgeon, I saw some incredible things in theatre; peoples' near death experiences, their souls leaving their bodies after death. I began investigating the connections between mind, body and soul. I set up controlled experiments on patients with incurable diseases and I made sufficient progress in proving the existence of the soul as a physical entity. I went to the board with my findings, hoping they would fund more research but instead they got rid of me. They said what I was practicing was against God!"

"It is against *their* God... but not ours. Our lord Lucifer cherishes your gifts. That is what you intend to offer him isn't it? The souls of the innocent in exchange for immortality?"

"Yes! Yes! You understand it. Once I am immortal I can prove beyond doubt the existence of the soul, the existence of higher beings, and that the afterlife is real! They don't see, they call me a freak and a fraud, but I will make them see! My research cannot be denied now, I recorded everything."

"I saw your diagrams and I found your machine. It really is extraordinary." Midnight played to Hemlock's ego by flattering him, all the while keeping him distracted enough so he didn't notice the flames from the candles growing brighter. "Tell me, how do you propose to make this exchange? The captured souls are in the theatre and I am here."

Hemlock's face broke into a devious grin and he touched one of the candle sconces behind him, tugging it downwards. The sound of stone grating on stone echoed around the underground chamber.

"There are many hidden secrets in this great city Mr. Gunn." He stood aside to show one of the recesses in the wall had opened to reveal a tunnel. "This tunnel runs from the church to the cellar under The Old Vic and out on to the river. No doubt it has been here a few centuries, you know how fond we aristocrats were of our escape tunnels. It turns out Mr. Wong used it for smuggling various contraband in and out of the city. Mary kept records of all her clients, but she monitored the dealings of her employer quite closely too. A very shrewd woman she was, a pity I had to kill her but she knew too much and I don't take kindly to blackmail."

"You had no need to kill Mary, I had already made her forget..." Damn! He hadn't meant to reveal more of his powers to Hemlock but it was too late, his excited expression said it all.

"My, you are powerful indeed. I have no doubt that this exchange will proceed better than I had planned."

"Did you take her soul too?"

"Alas, no. Mary was no more innocent than you or I. She was of no use to me aside from introducing me to the lovely Miss Rowbotham and being very good at keeping records."

"About her, why did you kill her and not the others?"

"I hadn't meant to kill poor Emeline, that was an accident. I only meant to scare her enough to draw out her soul."

"But then why murder Sally and Billy in my home? You already had their souls, you had no reason to kill them."

"Those people were destitute, they had nothing – no life, no prospects and no hope. What I did was an act of mercy! I hadn't the courage to kill them at first but then I saw them, hollow and devoid of life. I realised I had to be brave and finish what I had started. I was made to become something more than a weak human; I knew that the moment I began seeing souls in my photographs. I hold the essence of people's lives in the palm of my hand, I can decide if someone lives or dies, I can punish or reward. When I'm immortal nobody will be able to touch me and they will have to listen. I can clean up the city, the whole country, rid us of disease and poverty. I can harvest the souls of the dead in exchange for powers to do this. God will not help me, he has abandoned his people. Solomon used the demon Ornias to build his temple and so shall I!" Hemlock beamed at him. Clearly, he had chosen Midnight as his Ornias.

"What about the child? What will you do with her?"

"That child is as pure as the driven snow. My little nightingale, she will sing for me. She is my zenith. When I saw her selling matches in the freezing cold and saw her mutilated hand I knew she would be a great gift to my lord Lucifer indeed. A child's soul is special but hers, oh! If you could only see it; a rainbow of colour! But then you must know how special she is, it is why you claimed her for yourself isn't it? She put up a fight though, her soul would not come to me. I tried to force it out and I almost had it, but she blocked me and then I was disturbed so I had to make it look like I had found her. I tried to recapture her at the hospital but found she had been moved. I still have contacts at the hospital, it didn't take long to find her at the Asylum and then you turned up and put on a show for us all! That is when I knew little

Polly had brought you to me. She is my angel of death and her soul will be the sweetest of all to savour."

Midnight's eye's flashed and a candle flickered, he forced control of his fury. He must not alert Hemlock just yet.

"You said you would not hurt her if I helped you!"

"And I won't – if you keep your end of the bargain, I will keep mine. You will give me what I need and then I will release them. But time and tide wait for no one Mr. Gunn so if you fail in this exchange, if you kill me, you will never find them in time."

Quite suddenly everything made sense to Midnight; with the utterance of those words 'time and tide wait for no one' the pieces fell into place and he was sure he knew where Polly and Arthur were being held. Hemlock had told him the tunnel ran from the church to the theatre and on to the river. They must be being held somewhere near the exit of that tunnel, or even on the river itself, on a boat perhaps? It would have to be within direct reach of that tunnel for Hemlock to reach them in time to either set them free or kill them.

"Shall we get on with it then? I presume you have everything you need for the ceremony?"

Hemlock looked a little taken aback and unsure but quickly masked it. Turning away he reached into the tunnel and pulled out a black velvet bag. He took out a black candle, a brass bowl, and an old book which Midnight presumed was a grimoire.

"Where are the souls? I will not exchange power without them."

"We will go to them soon; first I need to bind you to me so you cannot escape. Forgive me but demons are not the most trustworthy of beings."

"How do you know, have you had many dealings with demons?"

"Just the one and he is a tricky little fellow. I have him under control now, he is bound to me also. I learned my lesson the first time I tried to capture him."

"So why didn't you just use him for the exchange?" Midnight was ready. He held more light power inside him than he ever had before. It threatened to burst from him at any second but now Hemlock had mentioned capturing a demon he needed to know what he might be up against in a fight.

"He is a lesser demon, not nearly powerful enough to grant my wish but he has proved useful indeed for capturing the souls."

"Impossible! A mere human and a lesser demon could not perform such a feat. Prove it!"

Hemlock seemed hesitant, even a little impatient but he could not resist showing off his genius, so he reached into the velvet bag again and pulled out a pair of steel-tipped gloves and a pair of eye goggles, not unlike driving goggles but with red lenses and wires attached. He put on the goggles and the gloves and opened his arms wide, then made a mocking bow.

"I give you the infamous Spring-Heeled Jack, minus the cape of course and its deep pockets that hide the jars."

"That's it?" Midnight scoffed, sounding wholly unimpressed. "Where's the demon?"

Hemlock sighed not bothering to mask his irritation he replied.

"In here!" He tapped the goggles. "It really is quite ingenious Mr. Gunn, you see after I bound him to me with his blood, I mixed it with powdered ruby and performed the spell he gave me. That enabled me to coat the lenses with that magical mixture. I released the demon back into his world but as he is still bound to me by blood and magic, I can call on him whenever I choose. It is his spirit that haunts these glasses. Once I have brought my victims to state of immeasurable fear, the demon calls forth their souls and I snatch them using these!" Hemlock raised his gloved hands and wiggled the metallic claws. "As I'm sure you know, silver enhances one's connection to all things spiritual. The souls are put in special containers and inserted into my machine where they're ready for the transference of power to me."

"A clever explanation but I see no demon. Bring him forth."

"I do not have time for this Mr. Gunn," Hemlock snapped. "Neither does your little pet. Now, enough explaining. Be quiet while I prepare the binding spell." Hemlock turned to a page in his grimoire, lit the black candle and began to chant. The air grew thick and heavy. Midnight was a little concerned; demon or not a binding spell would work on anyone should that person's blood be collected and used in the spell. His concerns were confirmed when Hemlock picked up the brass bowl and approached him.

"I need a little of your blood if you please Mr. Gunn"

Midnight bowed mockingly and held out his arm, wrist up.

Hemlock laughed,

"Do you think I am that naïve? If I cross into the trap it will free you and I'm not about to let that happen. I will throw you the bowl and you will bleed for me."

"I have no knife. What would you have me use?"

"How about your imagination? Tick tock goes the clock Mr. Gunn." And with that Hemlock tossed him the bowl.

Everything happened at once. As the bowl flew towards him, Midnight gathered up all his light energy and projected it outward, enveloping Hemlock in one huge ball of light. The bowl clattered to the floor, the noise of brass on stone was drowned out by the roar of energy that swirled around his enemy. He knew what he had to do now; Midnight called the light to him and it came, dragging a screaming, flailing Hemlock along with it. As Hemlock crossed beneath the trap, Midnight felt its hold on him break. The candles flickered and the ball of light that held Hemlock disappeared. The pair of them fell to the floor in a tangled heap as the shadows rushed in to their host's body and Midnight roared in pain. Just as he settled into the acceptance of the dark power he felt a sharp stab in his left side. Putting his hand to it, it came away bloody. He looked at the manically laughing Hemlock beneath him and saw that he held up a small knife. He had been stabbed!

Hemlock jabbed at him again, but he swept his arm in front to block it, the blade swiped across his wrist and he felt the warm flow of his life's blood spurt from the second wound. He let out an animalistic snarl and directed a blast of dark power at his enemy, sending Hemlock careening across the stone floor into the wall where he lay panting. Midnight got to his feet and advanced. He could feel blood pumping from the wounds on his side and wrist but he could not let go of the shadows to embrace the healing light, not until he had dealt with Hemlock. Just as he prepared to send another blow, Hemlock put the bloodied blade to his mouth and licked it. The action caused Midnight to halt his steps, with rising dread he knew what the action meant; Hemlock still intended to bind him. As the beginnings of an incantation reached his ears, he sent the shadows spiralling towards the man still slumped on the floor. One smoky thread heaved Hemlock from the ground and held him in mid-air while another forced its way down his throat cutting the ancient words of magic off in an instant. The goggles that Hemlock still wore began to glow bright red, transforming the wearers face into the demonic visage Midnight had seen in the memories of all the victims. The glow turned fiery-red and Midnight noticed Hemlock began to excrete a greyish mist. The mist slowly rose and took the form of its host; it was Hemlock's soul! So struck with fear at the prospect of his imminent demise was he that his own device had turned on him and had begun a harvest. As sorely tempted as he was to allow that to happen, Midnight refused to allow another soul to be lost. He would not lower himself to the same level of depravity as this poor excuse of a human and so he fought to control the impulse to kill. Hemlock landed on the floor of the crypt with a heavy thud. He was unconscious but alive... just.

"You arrogant swine! Be thankful I have not sent you to your lord!"

Removing the goggles and gloves, Midnight stamped hard on the goggles, crushing them. He threw the gloves to the other side of the room and removed the leather belt from Hemlock's trousers, turned him onto his front and bound his wrists together behind his back with the belt.

"I may be merciful now but I swear to you, if the girl dies, prison will not protect you from me!"

Giving him a hefty kick in the gut and satisfied that would hold the lifeless villain until he could alert Rowe, he set off down the tunnel. Swapping shadows for light once more; a ball of newly formed flame lit his path. Using what little of the light's energy he could spare to seal the two wounds, he ran as fast as he could, praying he was not too late.

23

THE BRIDGE

After five minutes of running he came upon another stone staircase like the one in St. Andrews crypt. Midnight assumed it must lead to the cellar of The Old Vic. He stopped barely a minute and debated whether to try and find his way to Rowe and send for help, but Rowe would probably be on his way to the mission house looking for him. He thought fast and decided he could not afford to waste time explaining things to whichever policemen Rowe had sent to guard the souls; Polly and Arthur were his priority.

Another ten minutes and the tunnel rattled with noise, he could feel the vibrations under his feet, *I must be underneath Waterloo station!* If that was true he estimated he could not be far from the river.

The tunnel ended abruptly and he found himself blocked by a large wooden door with iron rivets and thick hinges. The door was locked. Only dark energy would be strong enough to break it down, so he allowed the ball of flame to peter out, bracing himself for the pain of accepting the shadows once more. The door blasted apart with a resounding BOOM!

Splinters of wood and mangled metal flew outwards landing with a splash. Midnight stepped out into the night and found himself on a narrow ledge parallel with the river Thames. Taking in his immediate surroundings, he could see a rusty iron ladder running upwards to the street, to his left the narrow ledge ran along the embankment for a few feet until it met with a large iron mooring, beyond that was the new Westminster Bridge; still undergoing a substantial refurbishment. It was covered in scaffolding and construction materials and shrouded in patchy fog. To his right was nothing but the inky waters and a tide gauge painted on the stone wall. The gauge indicated it was almost high tide.

'Time and tide wait for no one', he heard Hemlock's words in his mind and fear gripped his heart. He could see nothing that might indicate where Polly and Arthur might be. Had he made a mistake? His hands gripped the jagged rungs of the ladder and he began to climb, perhaps something on the street may give him a clue. When he reached street level he found himself directly outside St. Thomas' hospital. Polly and Gredge might be inside; it was possible, given Hemlock's links to the place. Just as he headed in that direction something leaped up from the top of the ladder and landed right beside him; Hemlock! Except it did not look like the Hemlock he had met this night. This version had taken on a beast-like quality, his face had contorted into a grizzly snarl, its stance was predatory. Midnight noticed brown claws on the end of its fingers and its eyes shone like hot coals – no goggles or gloves in sight! The Hemlock creature launched itself at him, teeth gnashing at his throat. He barely had time to react, but he threw a bolt of shadow right into the creature's midriff, sending it right over the embankment and into the river. There was no splash so he hurried to the edge and peered over, expecting to see it flailing in the water. Instead, it was clinging to the ladder and it sprang at him again, knocking him to the ground. Midnight fired another bolt of shadows, but it leaped out of the way and bounded off in the direction of the bridge.

Bathsheba's backside it's fast! The creature had already reached the bridge and was climbing down the scaffold by the time Midnight had scrambled to his feet and made it to within ten feet of the first set of scaffolds. He barrelled after it. Launching himself over the railing and onto the platform, Midnight began to descend. The fog was rolling in and out in thick patches; one second he could see below him and the next it was pea soup. The blare of a distant foghorn pierced the night and on the tail end of it he heard the high-pitched scream of a child.

"Polly! I'm coming!"

Another scream rent the night air followed by a bellowing shout that sounded an awful lot like Arthur. Midnight jumped the distance from the platform he now stood upon down onto the lowest scaffold opposite him. He was near the waterline now, he could hear the rush of the tide below.

"Gunn! Here!"

He turned towards the shout, it was difficult to tell which direction it had come from.

"Arthur? Where are you?"

"Behind you, I can see you! Hurry!"

He spun round and peered through the fog and scaffold. He was nearing one of the arches under the bridge when he saw a glimpse of a face. Wasting no time, he darted forwards, balancing on a plank that crossed between the two platforms, he came upon Arthur, who was tied to a stone pillar and up to his midriff in river water.

"I'm coming!"

"No! The girl, he's taken her!"

"Where?"

"Look up!" Midnight followed Arthur's gaze and saw the Hemlock creature climbing back up the scaffold with the limp body of little Polly flung over his shoulder. "Go get her!" shouted Arthur but Midnight continued towards the stranded Inspector.

"I'm not leaving you." He said and summoned up the shadows to tear at the ropes binding his friend. Once the ropes slackened he reached for Arthur and hauled him out of the freezing water onto the plank.

"Bloody fool... he's getting away, should've left me!"

"Can you walk?"

The Inspector shook his head.

"Can't feel my legs... so cold."

"Dammit! Take off your coat, it's wet through. Here, have mine." Midnight tore off his coat and threw it at the Inspector.

"Leave me, I can't climb that bloody thing," Arthur nodded at the scaffolding.

"You'll be alright?"

"I'll live. Now hurry!"

Without waiting a second longer, Midnight scrambled back up the scaffolding in pursuit of the creature and Polly. He could not wipe the sight of her limp, bedraggled body from his mind, instead he allowed the image to fuel his determination to save her. He held on to that feeling as he chased the creature. Clambering on to a section of the bridge that created the middle stanchion of the central arch, he looked around for it. A guttural roar pierced the fog above. Looking up he saw it clung to the topmost platform about ten feet from where he now stood. Hemlock – or the thing that used to be Hemlock – bared its jagged teeth at him, strange snarling sounds came from its lips and he realised it was trying to talk.

"Give me power, or she dies!"

"If she dies then so do you!"

"I fight you, your blood make me strong. I have demon now."

Midnight couldn't fathom what had happened in the crypt to the unconscious Hemlock. Consuming his blood alone wouldn't have turned him into this abomination.

"What do you mean you have demon?"

"I am strong now, I have blood and demon but need power. Give me power!" he spat. Was Hemlock implying that his blood mixed with that of the lesser demon he had already bound – the one whose blood lined the goggles – had turned him into this monster? Could that explain the transformation from ordinary human to... this *thing* that stood before him now?

"Let the girl go."

Hemlock dangled the unconscious Polly out over the water.

"No! Bring her down to me, bring her down and we will talk."

"You lie! Give me power or she dies!"

Anger and frustration seethed within, tendrils of inky smoke curled from his fingertips. The creature hissed and shook the girl like she was a ragdoll, and Polly's head flopped from side to side.

"Bring her to me. Now."

"Power!"

A loud whistle rang out from the embankment, men were shouting. Midnight turned to see Rowe and two other policemen running towards the bridge. One pulled out a shotgun and aimed. Midnight flung out his arms and yelled.

"Stop! Don't fire!" But it was too late. The shot boomed out into the night and hit its target, peppering Hemlock's left arm. The creature jolted and screamed dropping Polly as it tried to stop itself from plummeting into the churning water below. Polly cartwheeled through the air, legs and arms floundering. At the same time the creature leapt from its vantage point, straight towards Midnight. Without a second thought Midnight sent a swirling blanket of dark power towards the tumbling child, halting her fall. He held her there, suspended on his cloud of protection even as the creature barrelled into him, slamming him to the ground. With one arm maintaining the plume of black smoke around Polly, he had only one hand left to defend himself. Hemlock's face was mere centimetres from his own, the creature's eyes burned brightly as it snapped its sharp teeth, attempting to bite. Midnight grabbed it by the throat, the dark swirls poured from his fingers and wound their way around its neck, slowly choking it. It was so much stronger than before and now that he was touching it, he could sense another entity resided within the body of Hemlock. The lesser demon that was bound to him now possessed him. It must have seen Hemlock's soul emerge in the crypt and with Midnight's magical blood inside him the demon could not resist possession of its master. Hemlock and the demon had been truly bound in body and soul now, the only question on Midnight's mind was how to defeat it? His powers had never been tested on a demon before, even a lesser one; werewolves and vampires he could deal with easily but this was something else. He knew he could never fend off his attacker while his power was divided, the creature was too strong, but he couldn't let Polly go and he couldn't let go of Hemlock because his throat would be torn out. More shouts from the embankment reached him as Rowe and the two other constables started to climb the scaffold. Midnight knew they would not reach him or Polly before his strength gave out; he could not maintain this level of energy for much longer.

Stealing a glance in Polly's direction he could see the girl was stirring, soon she would awaken and find herself suspended in mid-air by a dwindling cloud. She would be awake when she fell to her death and Midnight wouldn't be able to do a damned thing about it. His heart swelled. He had failed her. He would not be able to save himself and Polly. The Hemlock creature sensed his powers were waning and he attacked with renewed force. The beast bore down on him, the weight of its body pressing down on the stab wound in his side, reopening it. Midnight felt the warmth of his blood begin to pour from the wound once more, if he didn't seal it he would either bleed to death or be killed by this monster as his powers ebbed away with his life force. Determined to keep focussed on the waking child, he knew that if he should meet his end here and now, he would at least make it count. He would sacrifice himself to save Polly. Rowe and the two policemen were making their way across the scaffolding, they would shoot Hemlock again but that would not be in time to save the girl. She looked like an angel, her skin had a serene sort of glow to it under the moonlight... no, she *was* glowing! A rainbow of coloured light began to emanate from her, the sparkling essence swirled and waltzed around her, mingling with the dark power that kept her safe.

'Accept it my son, death is but a part of life, you must...accept it.' The final words of his dying father came to him in that moment and he finally understood. He watched in awe as light and dark co-existed, whirled and blended in a kind of ethereal dance, opposite yet the same. He knew now what his father

had been trying to tell him before he passed. Midnight had never fully accepted the dark half of him, he had always hated it, fearing what it might make him. The light energy had been more acceptable to his conscience but now he understood he must accept both as two halves of a whole. He would never be master of his powers until he stopped fearing the dark and let both powers co-exist.

As this understanding came to pass, the light from the few surrounding street lamps and the oil lamps on the moored boats on the bank flared brightly. Polly's rainbow shone gloriously as Midnight drank in the light's energy and let it mingle with the dark. His stab wound sealed shut and his body throbbed with this new-found strength. He pushed at Hemlock who sailed through the air, snarling and spitting and crashed into a platform fifteen feet away. Momentarily stunned, the beast lay in a panting heap. Midnight jumped to his feet and guided Polly to safety, laying her gently onto the platform beside him. Her eyes fluttered open.

"Mista' Midnight?" She managed a week smile before her eyes closed again. He knew he must get her home and heal her quickly but first he must deal with the monstrous beast below. He could not risk its return.

"Mr. Gunn? We're coming over to you! Where is he?"

"Below me, about fifteen feet away. I'll deal with him, you get Polly and Arthur!"

"You found the Inspector?"

Midnight pointed in front of him to the lower levels.

"Down there. He's in a bad way too, the pair of them are half frozen. Take off your coats and keep them warm till I return." He didn't wait for a reply but climbed down to where the creature still lay, its breathing laboured. He approached cautiously, wondering if he could somehow extract the demon from its host, allowing him to capture Hemlock and have him incarcerated. Despite all that had occurred, Midnight was not a killer. He'd let his powers get out of hand with Kim and that was something he would regret for the rest of his days – just like his father's passing. But, he had a chance to do the right thing and he must at least try. Focusing his mind, he concentrated his newly blended powers on Hemlock. He allowed the smoky tendrils and threads of light to curl around the body, marvelling at how easily he could now control both light and dark as one.

The body at his feet began to jerk and the creature's eyes flew open. As Midnight delved into the troubled mind of Hemlock Nightingale he sensed the demon's essence and pulled. The creature screamed with rage, reluctant to give up its host, but Midnight was too powerful. He yanked hard and tore at the demon spirit but it put up one last struggle. Just for a moment Midnight looked into the cold grey eyes of a very frightened and fragile Hemlock but the demon took hold and once again the eyes became two brightly burning embers. The beast pounced and Midnight reacted instinctively with a blast of power which hit it right in its core. It crashed into the stanchion behind and tumbled off the platform, plummeting into the freezing water with a resounding splash. Rushing to the edge, Midnight peered into the fog but heard no screams or cries for help, and saw no body floating on the waves. Just the fading ripples and a plethora of bubbles where it had been dragged under by the swirling current. He waited for half a minute just to make sure it did not resurface. Not even a monster could survive the Thames and its thirsty savagery tonight. The snow pelted his coatless body and he shivered. Shouts from above stirred him and he made the climb back up to Polly.

"Is he dead?" Rowe asked.

"I think so. Nightingale was badly injured when he fell. The river pulled him under. Did you retrieve the Inspector?"

Rowe nodded and pointed behind him where his two colleagues had made it back to the embankment and were wrapping Gredge in another layer of coats.

Rowe had covered Polly in his own coat but Midnight was anxious to get her home and warm. When he scooped her up in his arms he noticed her lips were blue and her breathing laboured.

"Go, take her. We'll deal with Inspector Gredge and I'll send word to the river police. Might as well make sure he's gone good and proper eh?"

"Thank you, Rowe. There is something else I need you to do for me tonight; bring the machine to my house, there are still people we need to help."

"Understood Mr. Gunn. As soon as we've got the Inspector settled in at St Thomas'."

Midnight gave the Inspector a final glance, Arthur nodded and raised his hand to indicate he was alright. He was headed for the hospital, supported by the two bobbies Rowe had brought along. Midnight knew he would be just fine but he would visit his friend later and give him a healing boost, just to make sure. He had no time to worry about what the two policemen had seen him do. Polly was his priority now. Perhaps he and Arthur would come up with some plausible explanation later; thick fog and snow, a trick of the light? They would concoct something together. He gazed down upon the girl whose eyes fluttered open and she graced him with the briefest of smiles. A shiver passed through her and Midnight responded by flooding her tiny body with warmth and healing energy. The blue tinge disappeared from her lips and her pale cheeks flushed a pleasing pink. A little handless arm slipped out from under the coat and around his neck as Polly snuggled herself into his chest. Midnight felt the rush of paternal instinct. He vowed that as long as he lived, she would never be without his protection and care. He might even go so far as to stay he loved her as much as any devoted father loved a daughter. Hugging her tighter, he proffered a gentle kiss atop her curly, bedraggled head,

"Welcome back Polly Peeps."

EPILOGUE

The River Police had searched every inch of that stretch of the Thames until dawn but no body was found. It was concluded that Hemlock Nightingale had drowned when he fell from Westminster Bridge. His dressing room had been cleared and the evidence filed. The newspapers had had a field day with the story, even though Scotland Yard had tried to play down the whole thing. Illustrations of the now legendary demonic killer flooded the tabloids and Penny Dreadfuls. Hemlock Nightingale had finally gotten his wish; immortalised – but only in fiction as the legendary 'Spring-Heeled Jack'.

"They're still writing about it?" Giles asked as he entered the study with a small parcel wrapped in brown paper. Midnight folded his newspaper and placed it on his desk.

"Unfortunately, it's proving a popular story. The public love a bit of sensationalism it seems. Is that what I think it is?" Midnight held out his hand for the parcel.

"It is sir. Shall I call the young mistress?"

"No, I'll take it to her myself. Where is she?"

"The front parlour I believe."

"And everyone else?"

"Also in the parlour."

"Better not keep them waiting any longer then."

Midnight took the parcel from Giles and hid it in his pocket. He felt a little nervous. He was about to do something that had never happened at Meriton house; he was about to host a dinner party!

The excited chatter from the parlour could be heard from the far end of the hallway. He adjusted his cravat and swept a nervous hand over his hair. The chatter dissipated when he pushed open the door and stepped into the room. He glanced at each of the faces before him; Mrs. Philips, dressed in her neatest black dress, minus the apron this time, Inspector Arthur Gredge and Constable Rowe, Charlie Fenwick the new stable boy looking positively proud in his new livery, and Miss Laura Carter who now held a position in his household as assistant cook and housemaid. Laura beamed at him and his stomach lurched, she was a pretty young woman who had blossomed in the two months since her recovery. Her smile was beautiful and warm and he hated to admit it but it seemed to raise a little blush from her when he returned it. Polly liked her a lot and they could often be heard giggling together. In just two months Midnight's household had doubled. It was lively and bright and altogether a revelation to him how one's entire existence could be validated by the love and adoration of a child.

"Good evening everyone. I do hope you are all ready for a feast?"

"Is there a goose? Oh, Please Mista' Midnight, please say there is!" Came a little excited voice from behind Miss Carter's skirts.

"Aha! There you are Miss Peeps. There is a goose and it is a big one! But, first I have a little gift for you."

Polly leapt out from behind Miss Carter, her eager eyes danced with uncontained delight.

"What is it?"

Midnight got down on one knee and extracted the parcel from his pocket eliciting a squeal from Polly. From his other pocket, he took out an envelope.

"Which one first?"

She pointed to the parcel and he gave it to her. She tore into the brown paper and a small leather pouch tumbled out. She wasted no time delving into it and pulled out an intricate pendant on a delicate chain.

"Ohh! Mista', it's ever so pretty ain't it!"

"Shall I put it on for you?"

She handed him the necklace, and turned around so he could fasten it around her neck.

"It's the stone from the bracelet ain't it?" She turned to face him again and patted the pendant. "It looks like an eye!"

"It is the same stone, yes. It is an eye, a special one just for you Polly Peeps."

"It's beautiful and all but..." Her lips screwed up as she fingered the pendant. "I ain't scared of your face no more Mista', it must've cost a lot 'o money to have it made."

"I'm very glad you're not scared of me any more child, but I should still like you to wear it all the same. That stone once belonged to a beautiful lady and now it belongs to another one. If you still want it of course?"

"I really do. I ain't never seen anyfink so pretty in truth." She reached her arms around his neck and hugged him. "What's the other one?"

Midnight chuckled.

"You're nothing if not blunt child," he offered her the envelope. "Merry Christmas Polly. I hope it's what you want." Polly took it, opened it and pulled out a document. Her nose crinkled as she turned it over.

"I can't read a bleedin' word. What's it say?" she blurted out, causing the room to erupt in laughter. Her brow creased and she handed it back to Midnight looking a little disappointed.

"Allow me," he said. "See this here? This is your name, and this," he pointed to a signature at the bottom of the page, "is where a judge signed to say that you are officially a member of the family, if you want to be?"

"What do you mean, family?"

"I have adopted you Polly, I thought seeing as I'm your legal guardian I might as well go the whole hog and make it official."

"I... I'm 'dopted? Like a father, like a real family?"

"If you want to be?"

Polly's lip quivered and she flung herself at Midnight. He scooped her up in his arms and the room exploded with applause and cheers. Mrs. Phillips was dabbing at her eyes with her handkerchief, Giles was clapping his hands with great enthusiasm.

"I take it that means yes?" Midnight whispered in Polly's ear.

"Yes, please Mista', I should like it very much."

"Welcome to the family Miss Polly Gunn."

"Thank you... Papa." She gave him an extra squeeze before she let go and was greeted with handshakes and congratulatory hugs from the household and guests. Giles poured everyone a glass of sherry for a toast and Miss Carter came over to clink glasses with her new employer.

"Merry Christmas sir."

"Merry Christmas Miss Carter."

"It's lovely what you done for Polly, you're a kind soul."

"Thank you. She deserves a chance at life, the same as everyone here."

"Charlie and me, we're ever so grateful too. The way you saved us, and then all this!" She waved her hand. "It's like a dream, I only wish... the others, you know?"

"I do. I wish we could have saved them all too. We did the best we could, gave them a good send off. Their souls are at peace now."

"What you did sir, it was remarkable, if you don't mind me saying. I ain't never known anything like it. Miss Polly says you're a special angel, sent to protect us all. Happen I think she's right."

"I'm no angel Miss Carter." He thought back to the demon trap Hemlock had used. *I don't know what I am anymore.* "Miss Polly sees the good in everyone, even a wretch like me." He smiled.

"You ain't no wretch sir!" Laura put her hand on his arm and he was surprised to find it pleased him, having her so close.

"Maybe not, but what I did was no divine act. Souls are curious things; they know where they belong. It didn't take much to reunite you and Charlie with yours. A little encouragement was all that was needed."

"Well, whatever it was you did, thank you." She looked up at him, her long lashes sweeping her upper lids and his breath caught. He couldn't fathom the meaning behind her gaze, all he knew was that at this moment she was the most beautiful woman he had ever laid eyes upon. She was mesmerising.

The doorbell rang, startling him from his thoughts. Giles was kneeling on the floor chatting with Polly who was showing off her necklace. He began to rise when he heard the bell.

"No, stay Giles, I'll get it." Midnight put down his sherry

glass and strode out of the parlour and down the hallway to the front door, his stride full of merriment and Christmas cheer. He had always kept himself to himself; fear of what he was, of being discovered, had forced him to shun company but now he found himself truly happy for the first time since... he couldn't even remember.

He reached the front door and opened it, a smile ready to greet whoever waited outside. There was no one, nothing on his doorstep but a package and an envelope. He stepped outside to look for the mystery gift-giver but saw nobody. Scooping it up from the step he made to return to the party, he flipped over the envelope which he saw was addressed to him. It was a Christmas card with a pretty bird on the front, it had blue and red feathers at its throat; a nightingale. Midnight stopped dead in his tracks, his heart beat furiously as he slowly opened the card. The inscription inside read; *'Season's Greetings'* but there was no name. He fumbled with the package, ripping the wrapping. In his haste to discover the contents, he was not careful and something tumbled out landing on the tiled floor with a loud rattle. Hemlock Nightingale's battered goggles.

The End

REFERENCES AND SOURCES

'Ode to a Nightingale' by John Keats
DepositPhotos.com

ACKNOWLEDGMENTS

To Ewelina, once again your patience, hard work and friend-ship has seen me to the end of another book!

To Lorna- druidy wingman extraordinaire! I literally couldn't have done it without you. Many late nights laughing about, researching and discussing all things 'Midnight', your enthusiasm and encouragement have been invaluable.

To Nigel, you are one talented guy. Thank you from the bottom of my heart for your beautiful illustrations. I look forward to working with you in the future.

To my beta and ARC readers, thank you for loving my story and characters as much as you do. Your enthusiasm, delight and eagle-eyes are greatly appreciated.

To all the people who support me and read my books, laugh at my antics, console with me in sad times, answer my questions and help promote my work- thank you.

To the readers, editors, formatters, designers, PAs, bloggers and critics- the Indie book community is nothing without you.

To family and old friends. To new friends, absent friends, and friends we have yet to make.

ABOUT THE AUTHOR

C. L. Monaghan is a self-confessed Scotophile living in the Kingdom of Fife. Writer of award-winning Gothic and historical mystery, and paranormal romance. Lover of hairy coos and red squirrels. Explorer of ancient ruined castles and beautiful glens. You can discover more about her and her books at: www.clmonaghan.com

facebook.com/Joesbookbar

twitter.com/MonaghanAuthor

instagram.com/clairemonaghan73

ALSO BY C. L. MONAGHAN

The Immaginario Duet

Immaginario

Andato

The Midnight Gunn Series

The Hollows

The Barghest

OTHER WORKS FROM HUDSON INDIE INK

Paranormal Romance/Urban Fantasy

Stephanie Hudson

Sloane Murphy

Xen Randell

Sci-fi/Fantasy

Brandon Ellis

Devin Hanson

Crime/Action

Blake Hudson

Mike Gomes

Contemporary Romance

Gemma Weir

Elodie Colt